A Passion for Poison

The Wronged Women's Co-operative: Book 6

T E SCOTT

Author's Note

You might notice a change in chapter point-of-view in this book. I have decided to let Liz Okoro have some maternity leave. She's just had a tiny baby, the last thing she wants to be doing is narrating chapters for us. She needs a bath and a family-sized bar of chocolate to herself for starters! Liz will still pop up, just not as a point-of-view character. Part of the reason for this change is that Bernie's niece Alice has been knocking at the door and demanding her own chapters. Who am I to deny her? I'm just the schmuck that writes everything down!

Yours, the somewhat harassed author.

Chapter 1: Bernie

"Fourteen quid for a candle?" Bernie tutted and the stallholder gave her a snooty look. As if the hippy woman could take the high ground. No amount of incense and fake gold jewellery was going to convince Bernie Paterson to spend that sort of money for a couple of inches of wax.

"When does the competition start?" Bernie's husband Finn asked, leading her away from the stalls.

"In ten minutes," Bernie replied. "Look, there's already a decent crowd."

She pointed to the temporary stage that had been erected in Invergryff Park and the people milling around in front of it. It was a dry, crisp October day, the sort of day that made you think autumn wasn't so bad after all.

"Don't see why so many people are going to watch someone fry an egg," Finn grumbled.

"Because they're celebrities, apparently," Bernie said, sharing her husband's sceptical tone. It was their son, Ewan, who had dragged them along to today's event. One of the competitors in 'Invergryff's Celebrity Cook-Off' was a social media star called One-shot Sam who specialised in narrating his video-game playing. Bernie didn't understand why he was so popular, but Ewan had been adamant that they come along.

Part of that might have been the opportunity for snacks, she thought, noticing that her son had sidled up to an ice-cream van. Finn went over to join him, already pulling out his wallet. Bernie checked her phone. No messages yet. She shoved it back in her pocket and wondered if her client was ever going to get in touch. They were always so eager to speak to a private investigator, right up until the point where they had to pay the bill. Then the ghosting began.

"Look what I got, mum!" Ewan grinned, a bag of candyfloss in one hand.

"I got you a coffee," Finn said, passing over the paper cup.

"Thanks." She took a tiny sip, knowing that it would be nuclear hot. It was. But at least the warmth was spreading through her fingers. It looked like it was going to be a chilly end to the year.

"Fifteen minutes until show-time!" A shiny-faced man with an ill-judged hairstyle called out from the microphone on the stage. There was a small chorus of cheers. Invergryff folk weren't easily impressed, but they would always show up for an event if it was free.

Ewan munched happily from his bag of bright pink fluff. "This is so good, why don't you let me have it all the time?"

"It's literally just sugar and E numbers," Bernie said, earning herself a glare from the man in the van.

"Mum doesn't eat refined carbs," Ewan told the man, popping another piece of candyfloss into his mouth.

"Or food colourings. Do you know how they turn that stuff

pink?"

"Beetles!" Her son shouted happily, pulling another piece off and squishing it down so that it fitted into his mouth.

Bernie shrugged. Boys. She should have known better. "Yep, beetles."

"Awesome."

Finn bellowed out a laugh and Bernie smiled too.

"He could probably do with the extra calories," she told her husband as Ewan wandered off to investigate the rest of the stalls. "He's stretching up the way at the moment, not out the way."

"I was the same at his age," Finn shrugged. "Hollow legs, that's what our mam used to say."

A woman with two teenage girls and a yappy little dog walked past. The dog was pulling at the leash while the girls and their mother stared down at their mobile phones. After a few seconds yapping at a bird, the pup walked over to Bernie and cocked a leg.

"I don't think so, boyo," Bernie said in her no-nonsense voice. The little dog let out a yelp and then jogged ahead. He put her paws up on one of the girl's legs, begging for attention, but she just told him off for getting mud on her jeans.

"Pity you can't get a phone for the dog too, eh?" Bernie called out. "Then you'd be all set."

The woman looked annoyed and confused, but instead of saying anything she went back to her screen.

Bernie's eyes narrowed. "I should go after that woman and let her know that parenting involves speaking to your kids once in a while."

Her husband tapped her on the arm. "Bernie, there's a bug in your hair."

"Noted," Bernie replied and she let the other woman keep on walking. After a recent argument during which Finn had brought up several moments where he considered Bernie to have been behaving unreasonably – the words 'cold-hearted bitch' may have been used – she had agreed to moderate her behaviour. As Bernie herself couldn't always tell when she was hurting the feelings of others (why did people have to be so sensitive?) Finn had worked out that they needed a code word. 'A bug in your hair' had been her husband's idea. Bernie reckoned it needed work. It made her think of nits.

Ewan had already wandered away to watch some kids with skateboards doing something dangerous on a metal fence. Bernie watched him go until something caught her eye.

It would be hard to miss the woman heading towards her, given that her dress was orange and the print seemed to be made up of smiling ginger cats. And she was waving like she was trying to direct a plane.

"Hey, how's tricks?" Mary Plunkett was wearing one of her more muted outfits today. Along with the extraordinary dress she was sporting there were golden hoop earrings and leather boots that looked like they were about to carry her off to a rodeo. And a multi-coloured scarf that hung down past her knees. It ought to have looked ridiculous, but even Bernie had to admit that Mary always somehow managed to pull it off.

"I didn't know you were coming along," Bernie said. She was happy to see her colleague. If they could get some work admin done during the show then maybe the day wouldn't be a total right-off.

Mary was looking around like she'd lost something. Bernie grabbed her elbow.

"The Dirty Beggar hasn't replied to my message yet," she said in a low voice. "And I've called him twice today but no answer."

"Oh, I'm sure he'll be in touch," Mary said airily. "Let's not talk shop today."

Bernie sniffed. This was not what she had wanted to hear, but Mary had already moved on.

"I've brought my neighbour. Do you remember Mrs Roberta?" Mary pointed at an elderly woman who seemed to be arguing with the stall owner who sold creepy-looking baby animals made from felt.

"Oh aye. The one from next door who wee'd on your fence."

"Ssh," Mary said. "She's pretty deaf but she can lip-read. And apparently it stops the foxes. Anyway, she was telling me last night how she hadn't been out of the house for a week, so I felt a bit sorry for her. I thought she might enjoy the Bake-

Off."

"It's not a Bake-Off," Ewan said, appearing from nowhere. "They're not allowed to call it that in case they get sued. It's a Celebrity Cook-Off."

"With a very loose definition of the word 'celebrity'," Bernie added.

"One-shot Sam is cool," Ewan whined. "You're just too old, mum."

"That is undoubtedly true."

Mary giggled. "And they've got that hot guy off the news. Nevyn something. The one whose hair is always perfect."

"Want some candyfloss?" Ewan asked her.

"God no, keep that stuff away from me," Mary said, making sure she was several feet away from Ewan. "Took me ages to get it out of my hair last time."

"Where's Walker?" Bernie asked.

"Working today. It's all hands on deck. Along with the autumn festival, there's a football match on at the stadium. The local derby so the place will be packed. He's over there all day."

"Good day to commit a crime then," Bernie smiled. "Maybe I'll go and pull the plug on the candyfloss cart if there's no coppers to spot me."

Ewan gave her a wounded look but she ignored him. Finn had

disappeared, probably to find somewhere he could get away from the chattering women in the manner of all husbands everywhere.

"I went to see Liz this morning," Mary said. "Couldn't believe how much the baby's grown. Liz says she's trying to crawl already."

"Nonsense," Bernie corrected her. "She's only three months old."

"Well, I think she's very advanced," Mary sniffed.

Why did people always think that child development was some sort of race? Bernie had given the new arrival her nurse's assessment and found her to be perfectly average. Just as she should be.

"Here's a tea for you Mary," Finn said, reappearing from nowhere with a cup for the woman.

"Cheers," Mary said, giving him a flash of her dimples. It was infuriating, Bernie thought, how Mary Plunkett could wrap men around her little finger without even trying. If she wasn't so nice, Bernie would be tempted to kick her in the shins.

"Time to take your seats, Ladies and Gentlemen," the man with the microphone said. He had hair that was pulled into a quiff at the front to try and look ten years younger than he actually was. It wasn't working.

"Thinks he's at the Albert Hall," Finn chuckled.

"Come on, I want to be near the front," Ewan tugged his

mother's arm.

"Is it starting?" A tiny elderly lady with a plastic bag in each hand appeared next to Mary.

"This is Elsie Roberta everyone," Mary said and there was the usual round of hellos. Elsie immediately started to quiz Ewan about the t-shirt he was wearing which had some grunge band Bernie didn't know on it. Skulls and guns still seemed to be the theme of all rock bands for some reason.

They found some seats near the front and sat down. Mrs Roberta pulled out a pair of knitting needles from her bag and got to work on what was either a very long sock or a very lumpy scarf.

"I'm surprised Liz didn't come today," Bernie said to Mary. "She's normally into all this 'support local events' nonsense. Remember when she took us to that cloth weaving demonstration?"

"I still have the gloves I made," Mary replied. "Problem is they've only got seven fingers between them. Liz wanted to come but she said that her mum was taking her and the baby out for the day. She said to pick her up some tablet if we spotted any."

"She's not going to lose the pregnancy chub eating tablet," Bernie warned.

"Bug in hair," Finn whispered. Bernie just rolled her eyes.

The be-quiffed man returned to the microphone. "I'm Josh Netterby, the Director of the show here today. Can I ask you

13

to all turn off your mobile phones? All recording equipment is strictly forbidden."

"Video piracy is a crime," Mary whispered.

"Funds terrorism, don't you know," Bernie grinned back.

"Can you put your hands together and welcome our celebrity guests for tonight's Cook-Off!"

There was a half-hearted smattering of applause. Netterby scowled at the crowd, then ushered half a dozen people onto the stage.

"First we have Loretta Shakespeare, former lead in the Scottish National Ballet. You might recognise her from Loretta's Dance School, a popular venue here in Invergryff."

A skinny woman with blond hair and a black polo neck stepped up to one of the tables. A few people clapped and some small girls in pink tutus cheered.

"To her left is Paul Gunn, our veteran entertainer who is currently the most-listened-to presenter on Radio Renfrewshire."

Gunn bowed before the crowd, exposing the bald patch on top of his head. The next couple of celebrities were introduced, before the young lad that Ewan had wanted to see stepped onto the stage. He did some sort of weird bow combined with a dance step where he touched the top of his head.

"What was that?" Bernie asked.

"His signature move, mum. The skull."

"He looked like an overgrown toddler."

Ewan pouted. "He's got more than ten million subscribers."

"And that makes him worthy of our time, does it? If you ask me —"

"A little bug there, Berns, just above your ear," Finn said, and Bernie snapped her jaw shut.

"Fine," she hissed.

Mary was shuffling in her seat next to Bernie in an irritating fashion.

"Can't you sit still?"

"Just looking for something in my bag."

"Have you got the receipts for those expenses from last month? We could go over them just now."

"What and miss all the fun?"

Bernie tutted. "Fun? They've not even started cooking yet." In fact, the crowd was starting to get a bit restless while nothing happened on stage. They seemed to be setting up all the cameras and staging, but not doing any actual cooking. Bernie was distracted by a munching sound nearby.

"What is that you're eating?"

"A Belgian bun. Want some?"

"You're worse than the kids," Bernie sniffed.

Mary laughed. "Got to set a good example. Besides, all this cooking is making me hungry."

"They haven't started… Oh look, they seem to be turning the ovens on at least."

"I used to have an oven like that in my Aberdeen house," Mary said, leaning forward to get a better look. "Cost nearly two grand."

"All fur coat and no knickers," Mrs Roberta said, a little too loudly.

"What?"

"Those fancy gadgets. In my day we had a coal stove and one pan and we were glad of it."

"Things have changed since the dark ages," Bernie reminded her.

"Cheek! I'm barely past eighty."

"What was it like when they discovered fire again?"

Mrs Roberta pointed her knitting needle at Bernie's face. "What do you mean by that?"

"I would have thought it was perfectly clear what I –"

"Bugs, Bernie, a whole bunch of them in your hair," Finn said with a note of panic in his voice.

"There are not," Bernie hissed back.

"Infested, are you? You can get a special shampoo for that," Mrs Roberta said, making sure to lean as far as she could in the opposite direction from the others.

"I blooming well am not –"

"Shhh," Mary gave her a smack on the knee. "The celebrities are about to start."

"Oh good."

Chapter 2: Mary

Someone had not thought this show through, Mary thought as the handsome newsreader held up a whisk for the crowd. Cooking, after all, was not in itself particularly exciting to watch. On the telly it was better because they could make it seem more dramatic, but the people on stage could only create so much drama by adding butter to flour.

Mind you, she had to admit they were trying their best. The newsreader, Nevyn, had just dropped his bowl in a move that she was sure had been staged. He had been helped out by a buxom soap opera star who had kindly shared her chocolate drops, earning her a smattering of applause from the crowd.

Paul Gunn, the silver fox who was on the radio, had moved to the front of the stage to show everyone his apron. A few older ladies in the audience did a whoop of appreciation as he hammed it up with poses for the camera.

"Ooh, is that Cary Grant?" Mrs Roberta asked, looking up from her knitting.

"Wouldn't have thought so," Mary replied. "Seeing as he's been dead for several decades."

Mrs Roberta shrugged. "Ach well, even the good-looking ones get wrinkled up and die in the end. You remember that."

"I will," Mary said, taking another bite of her cake. She had only gone to the cake stall to get a gingerbread to bring home for the kids, but she hadn't been able to resist a little bun for herself. As usual, she got halfway through the mound of icing before she started to feel sick.

On stage, the Cook-Off continued. There were six celebrities altogether and none of them looked like they particularly wanted to be there. The pretty young actress was whispering to the newsreader, Nevyn, and the social media superstar was already checking his phone.

None of them, however, looked as grumpy as the Director and Mary heard him ask a younger woman 'is this it?' and gesture to the crowd.

"I'm not sure Invergryff Park is quite living up to what they were expecting," Mary commented.

"Aye, probably used to Notting Hill or something," Mrs Roberta sniffed. "I went to London once. 1972. It was raining and it smelled of fish. Never went back."

The Director was at the microphone, gesturing to the crowd to hush. "Today we will be getting our celebrities to make that most tricky of dishes: the perfect brownie."

There were a few small oohs from the crowd, even though everyone knew that making a brownie was the baking equivalent of first base.

"Brownie? Another American fad," Mrs Roberta tutted. "What's wrong with good old-fashioned Scottish recipes? My granny used to make scones the size of your head. Tasted like baking soda, mind you, but they were huge."

19

Mary, who was rather partial to a gooey brownie herself, kept quiet.

"That lass with the bobbed hair was on telly the other night, wasn't she?" Bernie asked.

"Aye, she's normally in a soap opera over on STV, but she's putting out a single to try and get Christmas Number One."

"Can she sing?"

"No idea, but she was wearing a very cute woollen jumper on the cover," Mary said. "You know, I don't think they've thought this through. It's not like on telly where they can skip ahead. Now we've just got to watch the oven doors for ten minutes."

Sure enough, the men and women on stage were looking increasingly uncomfortable as they sat in front of their ovens with nothing to do.

"Who's the old guy again?" Bernie asked.

"That's Paul Gunn," Mrs Roberta said, looking up from her knitting. "He presents that Radio slot, the Country music one."

"Not really my thing," Mary replied. Her musical tastes were firmly eighties and nineties pop.

"He was a bit dishy in his youth," Mrs Roberta said.

Mary squinted at the grey-haired man. "Really?"

"Aye. Plenty of girlfriends, and more than a few ex-wives." Mrs Roberta cackled with laughter. She seemed to be enjoying herself.

"Oh, I remember him," Bernie said. "He was on Celebrity Squares once."

Mary took another look at the man. Sure enough, there was something familiar about him. She thought she might have seen him on one of those breakfast shows talking about his pets or something.

A young female staff member brought out mugs of tea for everyone on stage, earning a cheer from the crowd, which seemed to have decided that anything now warranted applause.

A whole lot of nothing happened. Every so often one of the celebs gave a nervous wave.

"Who will be first to open their oven?" The Director asked, with an increasing air of desperation. "Will it be baking success, or abject failure?"

Paul Gunn walked to the front of the stage. He seemed to be clutching his throat.

"Ooh, maybe he's going to start a sing-a-long," Mrs Roberta said. "Like Cliff at Wimbledon."

Mary wasn't so sure. There was something funny about the way he was standing, like he was worried he might fall down.

"Someone… there's something in this drink…" Gunn looked at the mug in his hand, then dropped it as if it was on fire.

"Is this part of the show?" Mrs Roberta asked.

21

"I don't think so," Mary said, craning her neck to see what was happening.

Gunn was on his knees by now, and the others had started to crowd around him.

"Something's wrong," Bernie said.

Without realising it, Mary had got up on her feet. "He's clutching his chest. You don't think…"

There was a crash from the stage as the man fell forward.

Mary saw Bernie stand up beside her.

"Let me through, I'm a nurse."

As Bernie surged through the crowd, Mary followed behind her, like those boy racers who followed ambulances so they could drive faster. She wasn't about to miss out on all the excitement.

People were shouting, standing up to get a better view and most had whipped out their phones. Mary hoped it was to call 999 rather than to video what was happening, but she wasn't too sure. It only took Bernie a minute to elbow her way to the front of the stage, where she pushed herself up from her elbows and vaulted straight up into the surprised crowd of celebrities.

Mary considered it for a second, then took the set of stairs that led up from the right-hand side.

A young woman with brown hair and a questionable fringe

stood up from beside the body. "I don't think he's breathing," she said, eliciting gasps of horror from everyone in earshot.

"Let me look at him," Bernie said, pushing her way past.

"You're a Doctor?"

"A nurse."

"Thank goodness," the woman said, her whole body sagging with relief as Bernie knelt down in her place. "I didn't know what to do."

"Have you called an ambulance?" Mary asked. She had sidled up from the stairs hoping that no one would question her right to be there.

"Josh, the Director is on the phone to them right now," the woman made her way over to Mary. "I'm Charlotte, the first aider, but I was only expecting scalds and burns. And these muppets have never cooked before so I've been working non-stop. I mean, I've only got seven plasters left!"

"I'm not sure a plaster is going to be much help," Mary said as she watched Bernie pull the man's body onto its back. She began to perform CPR.

There were more gasps from the audience.

"Can we do anything about his privacy," Mary asked the woman next to her.

She seemed to notice the crowd for the first time. "Oh. Yes, there are screens over there that we use to hide the camera equipment."

"Come on then," Mary said. They carried three of the screens over so that Bernie and her patient were out of sight of the people sitting in the audience.

There was something awful about watching Bernie slam her hands into the man's chest, but there was nothing else anyone could do. It was a long few minutes before they heard the sound of the ambulance.

The crowd parted to allow the two paramedics through. By now there was a large group of people around the man on the floor, and Mary stepped back so that she wouldn't be in the way.

She could hear the two men asking Bernie questions while they took over CPR. One of them readied the defibrillator and everyone stood back as they shocked the man in the chest.

"Steady rhythm back," one of the men said and Mary saw Bernie look relieved.

Another few moments went past as the man was attached to various pumps and contraptions and then he was lifted onto the stretcher.

Bernie had walked over to Mary. "Classic heart attack symptoms," Bernie hissed, too low for anyone else to hear them. "But he sounded pretty sure that his drink was spiked."

"Poisoned?"

"It's possible. But I think –" Bernie tailed off as the Director walked over to them.

"We're all to stay here," he said as the paramedics loaded the stretcher into the ambulance. "The dispatcher said that the police are coming too. They shouldn't be too long."

"What about them?" Mary asked, pointing to the audience. Some people had already wandered away, but many had stayed. She was irritated to see that some of them had their phones out and seemed to be recording the whole thing.

"Oh, yeah. I guess they can go." He walked over to the microphone and cleared his throat. "Ladies and gentlemen, as you can see we have had a medical incident. There will be no more from this event today."

The crowd began to disperse. Mary gave a wave to Mrs Roberta and Bernie's family as they headed away from the stage. As the other people left, Mary caught Bernie's eye. The nurse gave her a sharp nod. There was no way either of them were going anywhere.

Chapter 3: Alice

Alice enjoyed patrolling the park. Especially when it wasn't raining. Everyone in Scotland complained about the weather, but unless you had done a twelve-hour shift outdoors in the constant Scottish drizzle, you didn't have the right to dislike it. Today however was a chilly Autumnal pleasure, with the leaves a rainbow of colour and the air just cold enough to see your breath.

As always, she was enjoying the effect that her Special Constable uniform had on people. Most people looked vaguely guilty or gave her an over-bright smile and a nod. Some turned away so that she couldn't see their faces. She always kept half an eye on those people. The worst though were the busybodies that saw her as an opportunity to vent any and all gripes about the town as soon as she walked past. She had learned to spot these people and would often turn and walk the other way when she saw them coming.

Today, however, most people seemed intent on enjoying themselves. The stalls in the park seemed to be doing a roaring trade, despite the fact that most of them seemed to sell sweets that would be too sickly to eat or candles that were too pretty to burn. Alice stopped to speak to a few of them to check if there had been any trouble, but the local hooligans seemed to have stayed away for once.

If anything, it was a little too perfect. It was giving Alice too much time to think, and what she was mainly thinking about was what the hell she was doing with her life.

Of course, most people joined the Specials with the plan of signing up as a full Police Officer. That had certainly been on Alice's mind when she had joined. But lately she wasn't so sure. It wasn't just that the job was tough. She had known it would be from the start. In fact, the tough bits were the ones she liked best. The problem wasn't the job. The problem was her.

"Have you seen the state of those bins?" An elderly man with an even-more-elderly dog on a leash walked past, pointing towards an overflowing bin next to the playpark.

"Council responsibility, I'm afraid," Alice said, giving her Busybody Smile No. 3, the one that said, I care about your comment but it's outside of my jurisdiction. The man looked like he was about to say something else, but Alice had already strode onwards.

She checked her watch. Ten minutes since Laidlaw had gone for a wee. Hopefully, he would be back soon. They weren't meant to patrol alone on busy days like this, but when nature called, what could you do?

You were never on your own in the WWC, Alice thought, then shook her head at the idea. It was unfair to compare the two jobs, even if she had been spending more and more time working for her Auntie on the side. If the police found out, she would be kicked out, of course, and perhaps that was part of the reason she was doing it. Probably best not to examine that particular seam of self-sabotage too closely.

27

If she was being totally honest, the Wronged Women's Co-operative, despite its middle-aged sensibilities and ridiculous name, was simply a lot more fun than the police. It was amazing what a good time you could have solving crimes if you didn't worry about things like whether what you were doing was strictly legal or not.

But she wasn't ready to commit herself to the WWC yet. There were too many big personalities, and she would get pushed aside, left to make the tea and order the gins. And Bernie would be completely insufferable if she did quit the police, Alice thought. That was reason enough in itself to stay a little longer.

Her radio crackled into life. At first she assumed it would be Laidlaw trying to find her after a trip to the portaloos, but it was central dispatch.

"Assistance needed at the main stage. Crowd control and statement taking."

Alice turned back towards the stalls. It looked like the day was going to be an interesting one after all.

It took less than ten minutes for her to reach the stage where the celebrity cooking show had been taking place. Alice took a moment to catch her breath when she got to the back of the audience seating. Most people had already been ushered out of their seats by two elderly security guards who were now sharing cigarettes at the edge of the tent. The ambulance had already left: Alice had heard the sirens as she was jogging over.

And there didn't appear to be a single other officer at the

scene. Alice felt a flush of excitement. Of course, as soon as the full-time Officers arrived, she would be shouldered out of the way, but for the moment she was in charge.

Of what, she still wasn't entirely sure. She made her way up to the stage where there was a cluster of people looking anxious. Alice was already rehearsing her best 'allo, what have we 'ere' police voice when she saw something that made her stop in her tracks.

"Auntie? What the hell are you doing here?"

Bernie gave her the smuggest of smiles. "Stopping a murder. Aren't you a little late?"

Alice nearly bit through her tongue. "Can I speak to you for a second?"

She dragged Bernie away from the others, who seemed to be a motley bunch of crew and so-called celebrities. And an elderly woman who was sitting on one of the stools doing some knitting.

"What the hell is going on? And why are you here?"

It didn't take long for her Aunt to explain the situation. The man that had been taken away in the ambulance was Paul Gunn, a radio presenter and local celebrity. It sounded like he had had some sort of heart attack, but Bernie was already hinting about an attempted murder.

"He did say there was something in his drink," Mary Plunkett said, sticking up for Bernie as usual. Alice liked the woman – she was going out with a Police Sergeant, so there wasn't much choice about that – but she was far too happy to put up with all Auntie Bernie's nonsense.

"You heard him say that?"

"Us and a couple of hundred people in the crowd I would think. Plus they'll have got it on camera."

"Right." Alice left Bernie and Mary together while she went off to find the director, who Mary had told her was the one in charge. She found him with his head in his hands sitting next to six burnt trays of brownies.

"Can you make sure you send me a copy of all the camera footage from when Mr Gunn started to feel unwell?"

Alice handed over her card with her police email address. Netterby looked at it, his mouth turned down at the corners.

"It won't be ready to go out yet," he said.

"I don't need the finished version. Just any footage you have."

He shrugged. "All right. But it might take a while."

Alice was already walking back over to what she was already thinking of as the crime scene. She tugged on Bernie's elbow.

"Did you say he was drinking from a cup just before he fell over?"

Bernie looked smug. "Yep."

"You wouldn't happen to have seen where it went?"

30

"Yep."

"Auntie!"

The older woman sighed. "It rolled under the table over there. Just make sure when the big boys get here they know that I found it, not you."

Sure enough, there it was, still in one piece. Alice reached into her pocket for her disposable gloves and an evidence bag. She was lucky she had some leftover from the other week when they had had to help out with a particularly grim fly-tipping situation involving the local butcher's shop and a back alley.

She took a photo with her phone, then pulled the mug out, being careful to preserve any liquid that was still in it and placed it into the evidence bag. No doubt some grumpy crime scene technician would tell her she shouldn't have moved it, but with the amount of people milling about she felt it was the safest thing to do.

Alice stood up. There were still close to twenty people on the stage and she knew that she had to deal with them before they started wandering off.

"Okay everyone, I'd like you each to take a seat in front of the stage. I'm going to take all your names and contact details, then we'll start taking statements after that."

Luckily, her colleague Dan Laidlaw turned up at that moment. She took him to one side to bring him up to speed.

"Pity there's so bleeding many of them," the man from Fife said. "Any sign of the regulars?"

"Should be here any minute. I want to do everything by the book until they get here and start throwing their weight around."

"Understood." Laidlaw sauntered off to start taking names. He was a nice guy, but he never did anything in a hurry.

"You better take a seat too," Alice told Bernie and Mary who were hovering around behind her.

"What, with the civilians?" Bernie sniffed.

Alice was saved from responding to this by the arrival of two Police Constables. One of them she knew, a female officer called Kay Morrison who she had always found a little scary. The other was a very new-looking lad who could only barely be into his twenties with a shock of dark hair about a pale face.

"Alice, isn't it?" Morrison pointed at the new lad. "This is Constable Larry Brooklyn. Like the bridge."

Brooklyn gave her a pained smile, like he had heard that one once or twice before.

"We just got the call to come over here," Morrison continued, "but it didn't make much sense. Something about a medical incident and possible assault?"

"I'm just getting the preliminary statements, but it seems that the man taken to hospital, Paul Gunn, made an accusation that someone had spiked his drink before he collapsed."

"Is that a verified account?" Morrison asked.

"That's what my witness told me. The thing is, they were filming the whole thing. A celebrity cooking show live. So once we get the footage we should be able to see exactly what the man said."

"All right," Morrison said, a frown creasing her forehead. "Seems to me like this will turn out to be nothing more than a medical incident, but we've got to give the poisoning thing the benefit of the doubt."

"I collected the cup that he was seen drinking out of," Alice said, showing Morrison the bag.

"Good. That's a start. What about everyone else's cups?"

"I hadn't…"

"If it's a poisoning then we need to know if he was the only person targeted, surely?"

Alice felt her neck warm. "Of course. I'll get to it."

"Never mind, Larry can do it. You said you've already spoken to one of the witnesses?"

"The one who performed CPR on Gunn before the paramedics arrived." Time for a confession, Alice thought. "Bernie Paterson. She's actually my auntie."

Morrison raised her eyebrows. "Then we'll get someone else to take her official statement. Bernie Paterson, have I heard that name before?"

Alice cringed. "You might have done…"

"Can I speak to whoever is in charge," the Director said, interrupting their conversation.

"How can I help you, sir," Morrison asked her face immediately assuming the blank expression of a police officer dealing with the public.

"I'd like to get out of here. We'll have to start paying the camera techs overtime soon and today is already a total bust."

"Have you heard anything from the hospital?" Alice asked, reminding the man why they were all hanging around in the first place.

"No. I've called his wife and she's heading over there now. I guess when there's any news, we'll hear it."

"If you make sure that all your members of staff give their contact details to my colleagues here," Morrison said, gesturing to the others, "then anyone not on the stage with Mr Gunn when he collapsed can leave."

Laidlaw and Brooklyn left with the Director.

"All right, let's secure the scene," Morrison said. "We'll wait and see if they send a proper forensics team before we touch anything, but for the moment let's just safeguard anything obvious."

Alice walked around the set with the Constable. It looked remarkably like a certain televised baking show, but without the budget. On one side was a row of fridges, and on the other was the ovens. In between were half a dozen tables full of ingredients and baking equipment.

"Which was Gunn's table?" Morrison asked.

A quick chat with Netterby – who was still complaining about the overtime – confirmed that Gunn had been on the right-hand side of the stage, on the second table in from the wings.

By the time they had taken a look around Gunn's stuff, some reinforcements had arrived. Another constable and a non-uniform sergeant had arrived which suggested that someone back at the station was taking things seriously. The Detective Sergeant's name was Suzie O'Connor, Alice remembered, and she had long black hair that could have been in a shampoo advert, if it hadn't been tied up in a regulation ponytail.

"Sounds like you've made a good start," O'Connor said when Alice and Morrison briefed her on what she had missed. "We're not getting a forensics team for this. The hospital reckons he's got classic heart attack symptoms, so it's probably going to turn out to be nothing. But we're going to take some samples with us just in case."

Alice was a little disappointed. The kudos of being first on the scene of an attempted murder seemed to be evaporating. Still, she would be able to test out her training in evidence collection.

"Take samples of anything he might have eaten or drank," O'Connor told her, handing her a log book and a bundle of sample bags. "We'll put the evidence we collect on the spare table in the corner. None of the celebrities used that one so we're not contaminating anything."

The first thing Alice did was place the evidence bag with the mug on the table. She was glad she had thought to collect it first thing. Next she sampled all the baking ingredients at the table, making sure not to cross-contaminate the samples. Everyone knew a good baker tasted their food while they were making it, so it was possible that Gunn had been poisoned by one of the items on the table.

"Do we know if he had any allergies," Alice asked O'Connor when she deposited her tenth bag of evidence on the table.

"First thing the hospital asked, apparently," O'Connor said. "None known. Of course, it could be a sudden reaction to something, but that's pretty unlikely."

"Right. It's just… Hang on, where did my evidence bag go?"

Alice glanced back at the table where she had left the vital piece of evidence. Only it wasn't there. Two steps took her to the place where it should have been, but the evidence bag with the cup had disappeared. She checked under the table to see if it had rolled away somehow, but the sinking feeling in her stomach told her she was hoping for the impossible.

"Did anyone move my evidence bag?"

There was a chorus of 'No's' from her fellow officers.

"Has anyone else been in here? A cleaner maybe?"

"No one. Are you sure you left it there?" Sergeant O'Connor asked.

"Yes. It was the mug he drank out of, the first thing I collected. You saw me put it down, right?"

"Sorry, no," O'Connor said. She looked concerned. "I'll check with the other officers."

"There was a cup there. I'm sure of it." Alice looked around but no one seemed interested. "Are you all sure no one moved it?"

"No."

Alice bit her lip. She wanted to say something, but it sounded ridiculous. Because if she trusted her memory then someone had removed a vital piece of evidence. And apart from her, there were only four people that could have done it. And each one was a police officer.

Chapter 4: Walker

"I never meant to say anything about the lad's shoes," Big Sean said.

Sergeant Walker pinched the bridge of his nose. It was barely three o'clock and he could already feel a headache coming on.

"William here wasn't saying that you insulted his shoes," Walker explained. "He was saying that you verbally assaulted his wife."

"Girlfriend," William corrected, "we're no married yet."

"Sorry, girlfriend. William here tells me that you said his girlfriend was 'an auld pair that's cheaper than an over-cooked sausage'."

"He had just paid nearly a fiver for a sausage from the van," a wee man with trackies on added helpfully. "And it tasted like – "

Walker waved the man aside. He had no need to learn what the sausage had tasted like.

"Look, here," Big Sean said. "I never said nothing about his missus. I just said that about his trainers."

I am not paid enough for this, Walker thought. "Why would Willie here confuse you insulting his trainers with insulting his wife?"

"Girlfriend," Big Sean and Willie corrected in chorus.

"Girlfriend."

There was a pause while the two men glared at each other. Then the one called Willie shrugged.

"Well, I guess it might have been because of her name."

"Her name?"

"Nike. That's the missus's name."

"You're kidding," Walker groaned.

"No."

"I suppose it's after the Goddess Nike, right?"

Willie looked at the police officer like he'd just dropped in from Mars.

"Naw, Nike, like the shoes."

A few choice words later and the group of lads went back into the main section of the stadium to find their seats, still bickering as they went. Walker checked his watch. Three hours until he was finished his shift. It was going to be a long day.

"Did you hear about the celebrity thing?" Sergeant Neil Michelson walked over, eating a grey-looking hotdog.

"That's the cooking event isn't it? Mary was going to go and see it."

"Apparently they had some guy taken away in an ambulance."

"Really?"

"Aye. And they've sent a squad over to check it out. A full forensics team and everything. They think he might have been poisoned."

Walker groaned.

"What is it?"

"Mary was planning on going to that. With Bernadette Paterson. And if they were in the audience then I'll never hear the end of it."

"Is that the same Bernadette Paterson that got the council to take away the vending machines from the office as it was negatively affecting police fitness?"

"That's the one."

"Bet she did the poisoning," Neil said bitterly. "I used to love a wee packet of crisps in the afternoon."

"But you've lost half a stone since they took them away. You told me yourself."

"Half a stone of pure joy," Neil grumbled.

Walker had to agree. A late afternoon chocolate bar was one of life's most satisfying pleasures. Just one of the many ways in which Mary's friend Bernie seemed determined to make his life more miserable. He had no idea why Mary put up with her.

40

"Are you playing in the five-a-side tournament next week?" Neil asked.

"Hope not," Walker replied. "There's a seminar series about going plain clothes. I've been begging the Superintendent all week to put me on it."

"You still want to join SCD then," Neil said. "Be one of the detectives?"

"Aye. Don't you?"

"Not for me, mate. I like knowing what I'm doing and where I'm going. What will your missus say about it when you're travelling all over the place with the Major Crime?"

"I've got to get in there first," Walker said, avoiding the question. The truth was he hadn't yet explained to Mary what the implications would be of a move to the Scottish version of CID. That conversation could wait until later.

"They'd be lucky to have you," Neil said loyally.

"Thanks. But there's the... the reading thing. The Superintendent reckons it might count against me." Walker looked over at the crowd, not wanting to face his colleague. He still found it weird that most people in the station knew about his dyslexia. He had spent so much of his life trying to keep it hidden.

"They're not allowed to discriminate though, are they?"

"Not officially," Walker said gloomily. The thing was, he had spent half of the last couple of years seconded to Major

Incident Teams and he had started to see himself as part of the gang. He knew that he had the right sort of mind, the sharp way of thinking that would make a good detective. He just didn't know if he'd ever get a chance to prove it to them.

"Chin up, if it stays a nil-nil draw we might even get out of here early."

A cheer went up from the home stand.

"Or not," Neil added quickly. "Sorry mate, might not be your day after all."

Chapter 5: Bernie

Bernie Paterson had arrived home a full two hours after her husband and child. The possible poisoning of Paul Gunn had certainly enlivened what had been a rather dull day up to then. Of course, nothing was decided yet, but Bernie reckoned if it was proven that he had been attacked then the WWC would be in a fine position to do some prestigious – and lucrative – consulting for the police.

She hummed to herself as she opened the front door. In truth, although Bernie generally tried to avoid the soppy, sentimental part of life, it was incredibly satisfying to be able to use her medical skills to aid someone in desperate need of help. The man may or not pull through – Bernie knew better than most that the miraculous recoveries that happened on television after a heart attack were not always reflected in real life – but Bernie had been there when she was needed, and that was what mattered.

"How's the old guy getting on?" Ewan asked as she hung up her coat.

"No idea. They got his heart back beating with the defib, but we'll not hear anything now that he's in the hospital. Not officially, anyhow."

"I'm gutted I didn't get to meet One-shot Sam."

"Oh, that reminds me." Bernie pulled a flyer for the event out of her pocket. "I got this for you."

Ewan looked at the paper with the scribbled writing on it. "To Ewan Paterson, future gaming legend, One-shot Sam. That's sick, mum!"

"Sick is good?"

"Sick is very good. Thanks," Ewan gave her a hug, then skipped away to show his dad. Bernie smiled as she put the kettle on. It wasn't much that excited a twelve year old boy, so she was happy that she cornered the man as he was coming out of the portaloos, even if he hadn't seemed too impressed at the time.

Finn was in the living room watching the football. When the subscription to the sports channels had gone up this year, Bernie had argued with her husband that he didn't watch them enough to justify it. In response, Finn had worked out a detailed timetable where he watched football, tennis in the off-season and American sports like baseball at night. It wasn't often that Bernie was bested in an argument but she was impressed at his perseverance. Besides, it kept him out of the rest of the house so she could keep it nice and tidy.

"Hi pet, did they kick you out in the end?"

Bernie nodded. "Yeah. Alice sent me home. I'll get all the news from her later."

"You did a good job with that guy," Finn said. "Think he'll pull through?"

"I hope so."

"You all right?"

"Of course."

Finn turned off the telly and walked over to her. He put his arms around her waist. "I know you, Bernie, even you can't do what you did today without being a bit shaken up."

Was she shaken up? There had certainly been an adrenaline come-down on the way home, and she was glad that no one else was in the car to see her hands trembling on the wheel.

"It was a weird day, but I'm more pumped up than anything else. I mean, what if he was poisoned? I've been involved in plenty of murder cases, but I've never actually witnessed one."

"Am I a witness too?" Ewan asked.

"I guess so."

"Awesome! Do you want to look at the pictures I took on my phone?"

"I didn't know you took pictures," Bernie said, walking over to her son.

"I wanted to get some of One-shot Sam."

Her son handed over his phone. Bernie had relented and bought him one when he went to high school, even though she disapproved of them for kids. She had all the parental safeguards set up on it, even though she suspected Ewan could work his way around them in a second if he wanted to. Mind you, if he had managed to photograph an attempted murder, she might feel a bit happier about the blasted thing.

"Grab a pen and a piece of paper," she told her son. "Let's write down a list of all the suspects."

"Yes!" Ewan punched the air as he ran to get his pencil case.

"He's always wanted to help you out with a case," Finn said, his eyes back on the football.

"What about you, did you take any pictures?"

"Nah, I was catching up with the racing at Aintree. Didn't see anything."

Bernie rolled her eyes. Ewan came over with some paper and pens.

"All right," Bernie said. "Let's start with everyone who was on stage at the time that Paul Gunn collapsed."

"The six celebrities," Ewan said, his tongue sticking out as he wrote. "The best gaming pro ever, One-shot Sam, the news guy Nevyn something…"

"Nevyn Petty," Finn called out. "He's a Liverpool supporter."

Bernie didn't ask how he knew that, somehow he always did.

"And there was the ballet woman. Shakespeare. And the soap opera girl who wants to be a singer. Think her first name might be Rochelle. And there was another guy, wasn't there. Do you remember, Finn? He was a few years older than us, think he might have been a rugby player or something."

"Oh, aye, I'd forgotten about him. Steven Ludlow. They said he was a former boxer, but I'd never heard of him, so he can't

46

have been that good."

"That's everyone, then," Bernie said.

"No," Ewan said, looking up from his notes. "Hang on, that's only five."

"The victim makes six."

"The victim! This is so cool!"

"Okay," Bernie said, enjoying herself. She often felt that she didn't have much in common with her child, but it turned out they both enjoyed a good attempted murder. "Let's look beyond those six. Who else was there?"

"Can we look at the photos?"

"Sure."

Ewan squished up next to her. "See anyone we missed?"

Bernie flicked through the photos. "The only other person that actually walks on stage is that Director. Josh Netterby. He didn't seem that upset about Gunn. Seemed more bothered that his show had been cancelled."

"That doesn't make him a killer, does it?" Finn asked.

"No, but it's worth noting. He had a better opportunity than most to apply the poison. Problem is, we don't know that the poison was given to Gunn while he was on stage."

"We don't?" Ewan asked.

"No. Something could have been put in that cup backstage. So we can't rule out anyone who was working back there either. Write down 'assorted crew members'. I spoke to the Director's assistant, her name was Charlotte. There were plenty of others, mainly camera and sound guys, but I didn't get their names."

Ewan threw the pencil down in exasperation. "So we could have any number of suspects? It's not like this on CSI."

"I thought you were too young to watch CSI?" Bernie said, casting a glance at Finn who pretended not to hear.

"I thought I might study forensics when I grow up. Then I could be part of your Detective Agency."

For a moment, Bernie couldn't manage to speak. Then she said a curt. "We'll see," and watched as her son scurried upstairs to bed.

"Don't think I didn't see you welling up there," Finn said from his armchair.

"It was tears of annoyance that you let him watch inappropriate telly," Bernie barked, moving to the kitchen to do the washing up.

"Sure it was."

"I'm off to make a phone call," Bernie said, closing the door behind her. Enough of the mushy stuff, she thought, time to get her business head on and kick some butt.

Bernie dialled a familiar number. For weeks now, the Dirty

Beggar as he had become known, had been dodging their bill. It was intolerable to Bernie. They had done the work and now they deserved to get paid.

Of course, there was a good reason why the man was avoiding them. His real name was Pierce Mundell and he lived in one of the posh Victorian houses on the north side of the river. He had hired them to investigate his wife, a young Romanian woman called Mia. It had taken them less than a week to discover that Mia was the perfect housewife, never stepping one foot out of line. Unfortunately for the Dirty Beggar, the cameras that they had used to track his wife had caught his own infidelity with the kids' nanny.

Somehow or other, the photos of Dirty Beggar and Nanny Paulette had found their way to Mia, who had promptly hopped on the first plane back to Bucharest. Bernie had issued the usual invoice to Mundell, but he had refused to pay, placing the breakdown of his marriage at the feet of the WWC. Which was grossly unfair. Bernie had pointed out to the man that the breakdown of his marriage was due to his inability to keep it in his pants, but that hadn't gone down too well. Next stop was the small claims court, but Bernie would rather avoid dragging the good name of the agency through the courts if she could help it.

And so she found herself back on the phone with Dirty Beggar's secretary for the third time that week.

"It's Sunday night," the woman said as soon as she answered the phone. "And this is my private mobile number. How the hell do you know it?"

49

"Your boss isn't answering his phone," Bernie said, side-stepping the question which she would not be able to answer without revealing some largely illegal methods.

"I know. He told me, and I am quoting here, that he didn't want to speak to that lying bitch Paterson and that if she thought she was getting any money out of him, she could swivel."

"Well now, that's not very polite."

"Being polite is not one of Mr Mundell's strengths."

"I bet he's a nightmare to work for."

"He is," the voice on the other end of the phone said, "but he pays very well, so if you're intending to bribe me to bad mouth him, then you might as well forget it."

"Shame. Well you can tell Mr Mundell that our next step will be to instigate legal action. If he doesn't want his sordid private life splashed across the very thin pages of the Renfrewshire Gazette, then he'd better pay up in twenty-four hours."

"I will pass on the message."

Bernie hung up the phone. She was rattled. It wasn't often that she couldn't talk her way around someone, but Mundell's secretary had seemed oddly loyal. Maybe he was shagging her too? She made a note to do a little social media snooping on the woman. It would keep her busy while she waited for Invergryff police to phone her to come and save their arses on the Paul Gunn investigation.

50

Chapter 6: Mary

Ask anyone with kids and if they tell you they love mornings in term time, then they are bare-faced liars. At least that was what Mary Plunkett believed. Each Monday she got up extra early, determined that for once she would get a jump on the week. She would be the mother with the lunchboxes full of chia seed puddings instead of neon-coloured yoghurts in the shape of animals. Or the mother that waved her kids off with a kiss and a sing-song voice, rather than the scratchy yells of someone who is already five minutes late for drop-off.

Suffice it to say, by five past nine Mary was already red-faced and stressed, waving at scurrying children out of the window of her car. At least no one had died, she said, repeating her usual mantra. No one had died, and there had been no repeat of the infamous 'I don't want to go to school so I will stage a dirty protest' day. It could have been worse.

By the time she got back home, Mary wanted nothing more than to have a long bath and possibly a nap. So her initial reaction when she saw someone waiting outside her front door was to be less than thrilled. However, when she got closer and saw it was Alice, Mary cheered up. She had been thinking about the poor man at the Cook-Off since the previous day, and if Bernie's niece was here then there must be news.

"Sorry for dropping in like this," Alice said as Mary let them into the house. "I know you're really busy."

"It's not a problem," Mary said. "I'll put the kettle on." She was secretly rather pleased that Alice was there. When they had first met, Mary had found the woman a little intimidating. In her mid-twenties with the sort of effortless cool that Mary had always envied, Alice was the sort of person Mary wished she had been when she was younger.

"I've got peppermint tea and camomile if you'd prefer," Mary told the other woman, desperate to get in with the cool kid. She had a vague feeling that Alice's generation didn't drink caffeine. If only she'd thought to buy some avocados.

"Just a builder's tea for me please," Alice said, to Mary's relief. When she had opened the cupboard she had realised that what she had thought was camomile tea was a box of Kashmiri curry spice rubs.

"Did Bernie ask you to come round?" Mary asked once they had both sat down on the sofa with their teas.

Alice dropped her eyes to the floor. "No. I hope you don't mind, but I wanted to speak to you before Auntie Bernie. The thing is, I'm not sure what I think about it all and I need a sounding board. If I say any of this stuff to Bernie she'll jump to all the wrong conclusions. Or maybe the right ones, I'm not sure."

"Is it something to do with work?" Mary asked.

"Yes. The Paul Gunn case the other day. Something really bad happened." Alice went on to explain about the missing evidence bag. Mary listened in shock. From conversations with Walker she knew how seriously the police took the chain of evidence. No wonder Alice was worried.

"What have the bosses at the station said?"

"I don't know yet. I've been called in for a meeting this afternoon. I'm terrified they're going to blame me for what happened."

"But it wasn't your fault."

"Yeah, but who are they going to blame? The full time officers, or the Special that they can get rid of without anyone batting an eyelid."

Mary chewed her bottom lip. "What do you think happened?"

"Someone moved the bag. Either by accident or... well, I don't even want to think about the alternative, because if it wasn't an accident then why would someone remove important evidence?"

"If they were involved somehow. If they wanted to cover up for whoever did the poisoning." Mary shrugged. There were so many variables it was impossible to know right now. She wished she had Liz and her trusty spreadsheets to work it all out.

"Let's start with the possible suspects," Mary said. "Who could have moved the bag?"

"That's the thing, it's got to be one of the police officers. It was only me, Laidlaw the other Special and the three full timers. No one else went anywhere near the table I put the bag on."

"Okay, so it was definitely one of them. But why would they do it?" Mary asked. "Could it have just been incompetence? Could they have binned it by mistake or something?"

"I checked to see if it had been knocked under the table," Alice explained. "But it would be impossible to miss. It was a large evidence bag with red tape at the top and a mug inside. Not exactly inconspicuous."

The last few sips of tea went down while Mary considered the situation. "Tell me about these other officers."

"I don't know all of them that well. Sergeant O'Connor is quite young, and ambitious, so I don't think she's the sort of person to bend the rules. The two constables were Morrison and Brooklyn. Like the bridge. First time I'd met him, so can't tell you anything there. Morrison is a bit frightened, she's got a proper resting bitch face, but she's a good officer. And then there's Laidlaw. The other Special. He's all right. Not the sharpest, but he's reliable. He's our goalie in the Thursday night hockey matches."

"Sorry, did you say hockey? Like, the sport with sticks?"

"That's the one."

"Wow."

"What do you mean, wow?" Alice stiffened.

Mary sniffed. "I suppose I just wasn't expecting to find out that was what you were doing with your Thursday nights. I mean, of all things, playing a sport?"

"It's just a bit of hockey."

"And I thought we were friends."

Alice stared at her for a moment, before cracking a smile.

"You're joking, right?"

"Of course I'm joking," Mary leaned back against the counter. "I mean, don't get me wrong, the idea of doing exercise for fun blows my mind, but I'll find it in my heart to forgive you. Just don't start wearing lycra like your Auntie."

Alice shuddered. "Don't worry about that. The image is seared onto my retinas."

"Mine too. Do you know she dragged me along to a kettlebell class once? I tried to do that thing where you jerk it over your head and nearly killed some guy on the treadmill behind me. First and only time in a gym."

They sipped their tea for a few minutes in silence.

"I guess people see your 'look' and don't expect you to do sports," Mary added. "I'm sorry I made that kind of assumption."

Alice shrugged. "It was the same in school. The mean girls used to pick on me because I was into retro stuff like Jim Henson fandoms and grunge bands. But when we all played hockey together none of that mattered and they quickly realised that I was just as tough as they were. Kind of like when I joined the police. No one thought I was the sort of person to be a Special. Not even me."

Mary smiled in sympathy and tried not to feel too offended that cultural moments from the nineties were regarded as retro.

"But you've settled in as a Special, haven't you?"

"I'm not sure yet. And now all this business with the evidence bag… maybe it's a sign that I should quit."

"Don't let Bernie bully you into quitting."

The younger woman shrugged. "If anything it's the opposite. Part of the reason I joined was that she was so against the idea. But that's not a reason to stay."

"Maybe not. But I don't like this stuff about evidence disappearing. If there's a dodgy officer involved in this, then you need to keep being a Special. At least for long enough to expose them."

Alice sighed. "I know. Will you talk to Walker about it?"

"Of course, if you're happy for me to tell him. You're not on your own here, you know," Mary said, leaning over and giving the woman an impulsive hug. For a second she thought she'd gone too far as Alice looked a little shocked. Then she smiled.

"Thanks. That's good to know."

Chapter 7: Alice

Visiting Mary had left Alice with a brief warm and fuzzy feeling. Alice's own mother was of the Bernie Paterson school of thought, where houses were scrubbed clean and children were encouraged to be out of sight. Mary's house – chaotic as it was – was so clearly filled with love and personality that Alice wanted to put it on like a comfy dressing gown.

That was why she had felt drawn to Mary that Monday morning. She needed someone that would reassure her that everything would be okay. However, it only took the drive into town to the main police station for that inner calm to wear off.

Part of Alice felt annoyed that she was anxious at all. After all, she knew that she had behaved as she should, and Superintendent MacKinnon had a reputation that suggested he was firm but fair. And yet she couldn't help being aware of how vulnerable her position was.

At the station she was shown through to the offices of the higher-ups which were on a different floor than the main open-plan office that housed everyone else. Alice took an extra few minutes to straighten her clothes and make sure her boots were shining before she stepped into the Superintendent's office.

Superintendent MacKinnon had a ginger moustache and a posh Edinburgh accent that could have cut glass. Despite that,

Alice had never had a problem with the man. She had a feeling that might change shortly.

"Special Constable Paterson. Please sit down."

Alice took a seat opposite the man. It was hard not to feel like she had been ordered to see the Head Teacher. Something that had happened remarkably often in Alice's younger days. At least this time she knew she was innocent.

"I would like to hear your account of the events of the morning. I know that you have noted some concerns about evidence handling, but I would like you to take me through the entire event."

She brought out her notepad. Luckily it had been drummed into her enough times to make notes as early as possible, and she had written out a timeline as soon as she had left the Cook-Off. She was as prepared as she could be, but that didn't change the fact that something had gone badly wrong on her watch.

Alice passed quickly through her arrival at the scene, then explained what happened once she had started to investigate. "I collected the evidence before the other officers arrived. I followed protocol and secured it in an evidence bag. I held it in my possession until the others arrived and then I placed it on a table that had been designated for evidence collection, and then later it was not there." Alice had practised the speech several times and was satisfied she had managed to keep her emotions out of it.

MacKinnon tapped a pen on the table but didn't say anything

for a few moments. "Do you know if your colleagues recorded the same version of events? I mean, did they see you place the evidence on the table?"

"I thought it best not to speak to them, sir."

"Sensible," MacKinnon nodded. "Well, as you can imagine, this is a problem. Best case scenario, we're looking at human error."

Alice didn't like the way this was going. Not one little bit.

"It wasn't my error, sir. I bagged up the evidence just like I was supposed to."

"But you let it out of your sight, didn't you?"

She couldn't argue with that one. "It was placed on a table surrounded by police officers. I thought it would be safe."

The Superintendent rubbed at the invisible stubble on his chin. "It's a bloody mess is what it is. Now, I'm not saying that you're mistaken –"

"Then what are you saying, sir?" Alice interrupted, her patience wearing thin.

The man blinked. "I'm saying that we need to be very careful here. At the moment, all we have is an allegation of wrongdoing from a man in hospital. Unless we get confirmation that he was poisoned, it's just a medical incident."

"But..."

"If this is a vital piece of evidence, like you say, then there will have to be an inquiry. But I want to gather some more facts before I speak to Internal Affairs. That's the nuclear option, understand?"

Alice nodded. She didn't want to involve IA either, but she would rather have them rake her over the coals than let someone get away with stealing evidence. MacKinnon muttered on for another ten minutes, but he seemed to be saying very little. Eventually, he let her leave with the promise that he would keep her informed.

Of what, exactly, Alice thought as she made her way out of the police station. She was meant to be on-shift, but she didn't reckon anyone was going to stop her from going home early. The meeting with the Superintendent had not gone well. Alice could tell that he thought she was incompetent, that he was going to place the blame for the missing mug squarely at her feet. How much easier it would be for the whole station if the mistake turned out to have been made by the young Special rather than a 'proper' police officer. Well, if he wasn't going to investigate it, then at least she knew a group of people who would take it on for her. Time to make a phone call.

Chapter 8: Walker

Walker had been expecting the call from Mary all day. On Sunday she had only managed a quick call to mention the 'freaky thing that happened at the Cook-Off' before hurrying off the phone to get the kids ready for school. It wasn't until Monday evening that she called him and asked him to come over.

He practically skipped up to her front door. Sometimes it actually worried him how much he looked forward to seeing his still-new girlfriend. His single mates would be horrified. But the thing was, being with Mary was just so much better than not being with her. Even the kids – which, he would be the first to admit, were a bit of a challenge at first – had become so important to him it was impossible to imagine life without them.

He didn't even mind that when he hugged her hello his watch got caught on the tassels of her top, which for some reason had a picture of Dolly Parton and Miss Piggy on the front. He pulled her in close and kissed her on the lips.

To his disappointment she pulled away quickly. "I hope you don't mind, there's a friend of mine here." As Mary let him into the hall, Walker noticed a smaller figure behind her.

"Hi, Alice, isn't it?" Walker had only met Bernie's niece a couple of times. In truth, he had avoided her as soon as he'd learned of the family connection. If she had any of the Bernie

Paterson attitude then Walker had determined to spend as little time with her as possible. It had been easy enough as the Specials generally had their own areas to patrol and didn't often spend time in the office.

"Hi," Alice said. She couldn't have looked more nervous, twisting a ring around on her thumb like she was going to wrench it off. Something is up, Walker thought.

"Go on Alice, he won't bite," Mary laughed.

"Is it about you moonlighting with your Aunt? I know you help out the WWC sometimes. Don't worry, I won't tell your supervisor." Walker gave her what he hoped was a friendly grin, but it didn't seem to be working.

The younger woman shifted her weight from one foot to the other. "This is probably a stupid idea," she said.

Walker showed his best, most reassuring smile. "You don't strike me as a stupid person. And Mary wouldn't have brought you here if you were. So why don't you tell me what's bothering you?"

"All right. You know that I was working on the Celebrity Cook-Off crime scene?"

"I didn't. They don't normally use Specials for that, do they?"

"No. But I was in the area, and they were short-handed. Anyway, I'm pretty sure I found the cup that administered the poison. It had rolled under a table. I bagged it up, put it on the table where all the evidence was being placed and then… it disappeared."

Walker raised his eyebrows. "Wow. That's not good."

"No. And now the Superintendent is blaming me and it's all a bloody great big mess."

"Okay. Talk me through it step by step. How did the bag get lost?"

By the time Alice had finished her story, Walker was no closer to understanding what had happened. Despite what the public would like to believe, errors in the chain of custody happened remarkably rarely. Alice had shown him the log that detailed the item number of the bag in which she had placed the missing evidence, but of course that was only proof that she had written it down.

"I don't suppose there will be any camera footage or CCTV of what happened?"

Alice shook her head. "No. There's plenty of Paul Gunn collapsing, but by the point where we were cleaning up, the cameras had stopped rolling."

Walker ran his hand over his jaw. He was thinking carefully before he spoke. The thing was, there was a procedure involved that Alice needed to follow. And yet, even Walker knew himself that these procedures were not perfect. If the police force was looking for a scapegoat for someone who had screwed up, wouldn't a young Special Constable be perfect for that?

"What did MacKinnon say?"

"That's the thing. I'm worried he's going to pin it all on me.

He was trying to make out that it would be much easier all around if I'd just made a mistake, but I know that I didn't."

"Mmn," Walker could understand MacKinnon's point of view. It would be so much easier for the force if this all just went away. And it still might, if Gunn turned out to have had a perfectly natural heart attack. And yet…

"Do you know, I think that you should just go along with whatever MacKinnon says."

"What?" Alice and Mary both looked appalled.

"Not because I don't believe you," Walker said quickly. "The thing is, if what you've said is true we've got a very difficult situation on our hands. Someone moved that package, and I don't think it happened by accident or they would have owned up by now. The only alternative is that the evidence was removed deliberately, and by a police officer."

Mary whistled out a breath. "That's really bad."

"Yes. And if we've got a corrupt officer, it's going to be a nightmare to prove, and I don't want Alice getting it in the neck in the process. We can't take it to MacKinnon until we know which officer – or officers – are involved. And as soon as we make it an official investigation, they're going to know all about it and start covering their tracks. That's why I think the person best placed to investigate is you, Alice. You're a Special, which means you're on the inside, but at enough of a remove that you should be able to avoid being biased."

"Like a spy behind enemy lines," Mary said, with her usual flair for the dramatic.

Walker grimaced. "Something like that. Meantime I'm going to see what I can find out through the official channels. Sergeant O'Connor is a friend of mine and I'm sure she'll give me her take on it. I won't mention that I know you, Alice, and if you don't mind you do the same for me."

"Got it." Alice pulled on her coat. "I'm going to go home and grab something to eat."

"I'll see you at Bernie's house?" Mary asked.

"Yeah, see you in a couple of hours," Alice said, giving Walker a last tight smile as she left.

"I thought we were going out tonight," Walker said, trying not to sound too needy and failing miserably.

"We are. I've just got an emergency WWC meeting to pop into before then. It'll be done by seven and we're meeting at eight, right?"

"Right." He tried not to be annoyed that the WWC was cramping their style, as usual.

"I'll wear something skimpy," Mary promised, reaching up to run her fingers through his hair and suddenly everything was okay again.

Chapter 9: Bernie

Bernie had been ringing around her network of spies since first thing in the morning. Luckily she had two connections at the hospital. One was her husband's friend Ernie who was a maintenance man and general fix-it guy. When she called Ernie, however, he said he wouldn't be able to get anywhere near the ward in question, even when she tried to bribe him with the promise of a packet of tobacco for his rollies.

She had better luck with her cleaner friend, Natalie, who answered on the first ring.

"You still owe me a spa day," the woman said before Bernie had a chance to speak.

"I said I'd pay for that spa day if you got me evidence that Councillor Findhorn was stealing from the bowling club."

"And I got you the evidence."

"Evidence? All you found out was that he'd bought his wife a new car."

Bernie could sense Natalie's annoyed expression over the phone. "Aye, and you thought the same as me that the money had been nicked out of the council budget."

"Shame that it turned out the wife had won ten grand at the bingo."

"True, but how was I meant to know that?"

Bernie sighed. That was the problem with outsourcing. You just didn't get the usual calibre of investigators. The sooner Liz got rid of her breastfeeding bras and came back to work the better.

"Well, if you can do a little job for me now," Bernie said, trying to sound a bit more conciliatory, "then you might get that spa day after all."

"What job would that be?"

"Have you heard anything about Paul Gunn?"

"Is that the bloke off the radio? He came into the hospital yesterday. Heart attack, wasn't it?"

"Possibly," Bernie said, not wanting to give too much away. Natalie was a money-grabber, which was why she made such a useful snitch, but the woman wouldn't hesitate to sell a story to the paper if she thought there was fifty quid in it. Or a spa day with an Indian head massage. "Don't suppose you've been anywhere near him?"

"Nah, not been on that ward."

"Think you can arrange some time there over the next few days."

"No problem," Natalie said. "Anything else?"

"Find out who's been visiting him. I'd like a list of names. And any... unusual symptoms that he might have had. Any rumours about his health, that sort of thing. Oh, and most important, as soon as he wakes up you phone and let me know."

"Got it. Anyway, I already know who's been visiting him, coz my mate Ryan saw them."

"Who?"

"The girl that's doing that terrible Mariah Carey cover. You know, the Christmas song. Only they wouldn't let her in because she's not next of kin. She was having a right barny with the nurse over it."

"Rochelle Mitchell? I didn't know they were that friendly," Bernie said, making a note on her pad. "Thanks for that. Any other intel going around?"

"Just about Doctor Simpson's new girlfriend who turns out to also be Doctor Khan's girlfriend. But that's probably not relevant."

"Probably not." Bernie wrote down the names anyway. You never knew who might hire you to investigate an infidelity so it was always worth knowing the seedy gossip.

Another three reminders about the spa day and Bernie managed to get Natalie off the phone just as Mary Plunkett walked in the door.

"Finn let me in. He's going out to the pub."

"Getting away from us, more like," Bernie said. "I told him I'm mad at Alice and he thinks there's going to be a big row."

"Why would you be mad at Alice?"

"She only told me an hour ago about the missing evidence. I suppose she already told you?"

"Only because she wanted me to get in touch with Walker for her."

"Walker?" Bernie folded her arms. "What use is a copper going to be to catch a bent copper?"

"You sound like someone off *The Sweeney*," Mary grumbled.

"I was going for *Line of Duty*, but fine, it doesn't matter. Do you really think your boyfriend is going to be able to investigate his pals?"

"I'm sure he'll do just fine," Mary said. "I brought some gin with me and some of those sour cream rice cakes that you like."

"I'm intermittent fasting at the moment. High protein during the day and not even a lentil chip after seven o'clock."

Mary looked horrified. "Bernie, you barely eat anything as it is."

"I put on half a kilo last week," Bernie told her.

"That's not much, is it?"

It was so difficult to explain these things to people that simply would not attempt to understand weight loss. People that had never been so big they had got stuck in a seat in the Big Dipper at Blackpool and had to go around three times before someone could pull them out. And then vowed that they would never,

ever, go back to that indignity.

"It's not the amount. It's the trend. I need to nip it in the bud."

"Right. But you know that no one cares if you put on a bit of weight?"

"Maybe not. But I remember carrying around the weight of an extra person on my back. And my shoulders and my knees. It was not a happy time."

Mary sighed. "So that's why you've gone high protein?"

"Yes. And I've signed up for an Iron Man tournament next month. Time for a new challenge."

"Is that that thing where you have to eat as many hotdogs as possible?"

Bernie was about to go off on one until she noticed that Mary was already giggling. She threw a lentil chip at her friend.

"Very funny. I'm hoping I can beat at least half the men that enter."

"That would be worth seeing."

The doorbell rang and Bernie went to let her niece in.

"Hi Auntie," she said. "I hear you're annoyed with me. Again."

"Who tipped you off?"

70

"Ewan texted me on his dad's phone."

"The little traitor!" Bernie's son was at a sleepover, but she would be giving him a little reminder of the importance of loyalty when he came home.

"He just wanted to warn me, that's all. Thing is, I've had a monumentally crappy day, so if you're going to have a go at me, can we just get it out of the way now?"

Bernie looked at her niece's tired face and felt rather deflated. "Well, let's just say you've learned your lesson, okay?"

"Whatever the lesson was, I've learned it. Now, has anyone got anything to drink?"

After she had been suitably supplied with some American beer, Alice told them about her meeting with MacKinnon. Bernie was outraged on her behalf.

"I knew those idiots at the station couldn't find their arses with their own hands. He's just hoping that Paul Gunn makes a miraculous recovery and this all goes away quietly. Idiot!"

"Have we heard any updates on how Gunn is doing?" Mary asked.

"Nothing," Bernie said and Alice shook her head.

"Unlike the boys at Invergryff police station, I think we should assume this is an attempted murder and go from there."

"Thanks Auntie," Alice said, "it means a lot that you're helping me out."

"You're one of us," Bernie said firmly. "Now don't get all wet lettuce about it. You look done in already. You go home and get a good sleep and Mary and I will do some brainstorming."

After Alice left, Bernie turned to Mary. "Alice might be in real trouble here. I think we need our best mind on the job, and that's Liz. No offense."

"I don't think we should keep interrupting her maternity leave," Mary said.

"We'll be doing her a favour. She's probably bored stiff."

"I'm not sure 'bored' is how I'd describe the utter hell of looking after a newborn."

Bernie blinked. "Hell? Sure, it's not rocket science is it?"

"Let me guess, your Ewan slept right the way through?"

"From four weeks old. You just need a bit of discipline, that's all."

For some reason Mary didn't answer that one.

Chapter 10: Mary

Mary had left Bernie's house and headed home after one gin. Still, the woman had called her mobile before Mary had even had a chance to get into her sluttiest dress. Bernie hadn't taken any hints and was still talking about WWC business. As Mary was meant to be meeting Walker in half an hour it meant that she was currently shaving her legs in the sink with the phone on speaker.

"I've got Liz doing the accounts for this quarter. I got her to send me your expense claims."

"Right," Mary said, waiting for the oncoming storm.

"Seems to me that there's a lot of spending here at coffee shops."

"You had me on four stakeouts last month. How else am I meant to watch people apart from in cafés?"

"I'll pay for the coffees, but not the cakes."

"Slave driver," Mary grumbled.

"What was that?"

"Nothing. Heard anything more about Paul Gunn?"

"Not woken up yet. I've got my sources at the hospital keeping an eye on him, so we'll find out if anything changes. Maybe if the poor man dies then the police will start listening to us."

"Hopefully it won't come to that," Mary said. She was only half paying attention as she was wondering whether to wear the pink dress that made her feel like Buffy, or the black dress that made her feel like Faith. How to choose?

"In other news, I'm getting nowhere with the Dirty Beggar," Bernie told her.

"Are you thinking court?"

Her friend sighed. "I'd rather not. Normally I can manage to persuade people to pay up, but I can't get near the old fraud."

Mary folded a couple of t-shirts and shoved them into a drawer. "I'm sure you'll get him in the end. What did you think about what Alice said? Do you think we've got a police officer involved in the whole poisoning thing?"

"It's possible. And if it is then we'll have to make damn sure that our evidence is watertight. The whole of Police Scotland will be against us."

Mary couldn't miss the relish in Bernie's voice.

"You'd love to take them on, wouldn't you?"

Her friend laughed. "You know I would. It wouldn't be the first time that we've beaten them at their own game."

"Look Bernie, I need to go," Mary said. "For once, my mum is taking the kids and I'm going to manage a dinner out with Walker. I've got my fanciest bra on. I can't wait."

Mary put down the phone, only for it to ring again immediately.

"Hi mum, everything okay?"

"Lauren is sick," Nel said. "I'm really sorry, but she's been crying for you for an hour already. I don't suppose you could come and pick her up?"

Mary allowed herself the tiniest of sighs. "Of course. I'll be right over."

It only took five minutes to drive to her mum's house. As soon as Mary saw the look on Nel's face, she knew she had made the right decision.

"Her temp is right up there," Nel was wringing her hands together. "I wouldn't have called you otherwise. I'm sorry about your big date."

"It's all right, Walker will understand," Mary said. She had found Lauren on the sofa watching a cartoon. Her forehead felt hot and her eyelids were drooping. Mary scooped her up in her arms.

"Do you want me to keep the others overnight?"

"Just drop them back at bedtime," she told her mum. "I'll bank the overnight babysitting for another time."

"Your policeman friend won't mind?"

Mary laughed. "We've been going out for long enough he's used to it. I think he likes it that I can't complain when his work makes him do overtime. We cancel on each other so often we've stopped keeping score."

"And you've not thought about making things a bit more official."

"What, moving in together? There's barely room to swing a cat in my place as it is!"

Nel pursed her lips. "Actually, I was thinking about marriage. It's good for kids to have a stable home."

"And my home is a little wobbly, is that it?"

"No. But…"

"Mum, I've just got out of one marriage. I've no urge to go headfirst into another one."

"I suppose you're right," Nel said, holding the door open so that Mary could manoeuvre Lauren into her car seat. "I just want you to be settled."

Mary was trying her best not to feel attacked, but her patience was wearing thin. "I am settled. Me and the kids are doing just fine. And Walker, well, we're keeping things casual."

"All right. Let me know how Lauren is in the morning."

"Of course." Mary waved to her mother and drove away. She looked at her reflection in the rear-view mirror. It was the face of a liar. There was nothing in the slightest bit casual about her relationship with Walker. On her side at least. But there was no harm in letting her mother think that.

Chapter 11: Alice

Dan Laidlaw's flat was in a nice area, just outside of the centre of town. It was a cottage flat, the bottom corner of a block of four. The garden looked rather neglected and the hedge could have done with a trim. Not surprising really. Laidlaw's day job was as a bus driver, so between that and his commitments to the Specials he probably didn't have too much time for garden maintenance.

Alice had been there once before, for a rugby night when Laidlaw had invited a group of the hockey team around to watch his big flat-screen. Not that into rugby, Alice had been pretty bored and had ended up making an excuse to leave at half-time. Still, it had been nice of him to invite her. That was just the sort of guy he was – nice. Not the sort of guy to mess with evidence, she would have bet her life on it. But she would have said the same about all the rest, so who knew?

Feeling nervous, she pushed the doorbell.

"What are you doing here?" Laidlaw did not look pleased to see her. He was wearing old jeans that showed more than a little of his middle-age spread above the waistband.

"I wanted a chat about yesterday."

"Look, it's probably for the best if you're not seen here. We don't want to be accused of fixing our stories."

"You're wanting rid of me, is that it?" Alice felt her frustration rise. "Jesus, Dan, I'm not that much of an outcast already, am I?"

He ran his hand over his bald head. "No, of course not. Look, why don't you come in and I'll make you a cuppa."

Mollified, Alice followed him into the flat. Just like she remembered, it was small but neat as a pin with the main room dominated by a massive telly. A bachelor pad, but quite a nice one. Alice, who still lived with her mum, was quite envious.

"Going out on the bike today?" Alice asked. Dan was a fan of vintage motorcycles and had one stored at a garage in town.

"Might do if the weather stays good. I'm on the busses at four."

"Right. Well, I don't quite know how to say this, but I want to ask you if you saw what happened to that evidence bag on Sunday. I know that it's the talk of the station, but you were there. Did you see anything?"

"I never even saw the bloody thing in the first place, let alone seeing someone nick it. I was doing the interviews, remember?"

Alice creased her forehead trying to picture the scene. "But you came and helped with the evidence gathering, didn't you?"

"Not until later. Are you sure you put the thing where you said you did? Maybe you left it somewhere on the stage and someone else grabbed it."

"I'm sure," Alice said firmly. "You know me, I'm not a sloppy worker."

"I know, but you're still a newbie. Do you want a wee bit of advice? When they call you in for a formal interview, just 'no comment' the whole thing."

"But I haven't done anything wrong!"

"I know. But once the wheels of the machine start going, someone is going to get squashed underneath. And it's looking like it's going to be you."

Alice bit her lip in frustration. She had looked up to Laidlaw when they had started working together. He had been a Special for nearly a decade and he'd taught her the rules, both official and unofficial. And now he was telling her to keep her mouth shut and let her job go down the toilet.

"Why don't you just get out?" Laidlaw asked, as if reading her mind. "You've finished your college course now. You've got your Aunt's agency. You can do anything you want. No point in being stuck here for the rest of your life, is there?"

"I don't look at it like that," Alice said.

"Come on, the Specials was only ever a box to tick on your CV. Someone like you would never want to do it long term."

There was a long pause after that statement while Alice tried to keep her temper in check. And failed.

"Someone like me? What, too young? Too female?"

"Too goth!" Laidlaw yelled, then put a hand to his mouth like a

79

small child. He made such a comical picture that Alice found herself bursting into laughter. After a few shocked seconds Laidlaw did the same.

"I'm sorry," he said, once they had both stopped laughing. "That came out all wrong. I just meant to say that, even if this blows up in your face, you'll be fine. You're a smart girl with enough experience and qualifications you could do anything. Not like the rest of us idiots."

"I'm not going to let them force me out," Alice said, her dark mood returning. "And besides, this is bigger than me. If I'm right, someone removed vital evidence in a possible murder case."

Laidlaw shook his head so much it looked like it might fall off. "I'm sure it's just that someone screwed up. Thought it was rubbish and put it in the bin or something. I know all the officers that were there that day and there's not one of them that would jeopardise a case deliberately."

Alice wished she could be so sure, but she didn't say anything. It was clear that Laidlaw had already made up his mind as to what had happened.

"I'm going to want to talk to you again," Alice said as she made her way towards the door.

"Of course."

"And you'll back me up at the station if anyone asks?"

"Sure," he said as he let her out of the door. But she noticed that he hadn't met her eyes as he'd said it. Alice knew that as far as Dan Laidlaw was concerned, she was on her own.

Chapter 12: Walker

Walker was not feeling at his best. Mary had cancelled his date last night, for a totally valid reason, but he had still been disappointed. He had drowned his sorrows a little too hard. Funnily enough, since his army days he had pretty much come off the booze altogether. The hangovers now that he was on the wrong side of thirty simply weren't worth it. But last night he had opened a bottle of wine, and then another.

At least he wasn't at work with this hangover. That had been another thing that had led him to embrace the bottle. He had asked the Superintendent if he could attend the training sessions this week being run by the SCD. It was a widely held opinion that the more you showed your face at these sorts of things, the more likely it was that you might get picked for the move to plain clothes.

But when Walker had checked the rota, he wasn't on at the times of the training, and that seemed to be that. And now Alice was telling him that he might be working with a corrupt cop. It didn't rain but it poured, as it seemed to do all the time in Invergryff.

To pull himself out of his funk, he put on his trainers and went out for a run. Unlike many of his co-workers, Walker didn't particularly enjoy going to the gym. He'd much rather get his exercise in with a bit of fresh air and some vintage hip-hop tunes coming through his earphones to keep his pace up.

He pulled his cap down low so that if any crimes were being committed he wouldn't have to see them, and started his usual half hour circuit of the area.

Walker would never set any speed records since his knees were not what they once were, but as soon as he started running he could feel the hangover slipping away.

A call came through on his mobile and Walker answered it with his hands-free set.

"Hello?"

"It's Suzie. I heard you were wanting to speak to me."

Walker slowed down to a stop at a park bench. "That's right. I wanted to ask you about that business on Sunday with the radio presenter."

"You're not assigned to the case, are you?"

"No, but you know that Mary and Bernie were there," Walker said, being careful to keep Alice's name out of it. "It would be nice to get Bernie off my back if I could feed them some updates. Nothing confidential, of course."

"Well, there's no updates so far confidential or not. Paul Gunn is still unconscious and the hospital hasn't told us what's in his system yet, so as far as we know it's just a medical incident."

"I heard there was some story about evidence going walkabout."

"You heard that, did you?" Walker could hear the irritation in her voice. "I suppose bad news gets around quickly. I'm hoping it was just a misunderstanding. I never saw any evidence bag, although the Special is convinced there was one."

"Is she?"

"Yeah, and she doesn't seem like the sort of dozy type to make it up. So I'm keeping an open mind."

"Any findings on the evidence that was collected?" Walker asked.

"None of it has been processed yet. There's not much point until we've got reasonable cause to believe that there is something going on here. Can you imagine the Super's face if we maxed out the budget and it turned out the old guy had a heart attack? MacKinnon's orders are to take statements and do the minimum until we hear anything different. To be honest, I can't disagree with him."

"Fair enough," Walker said. "Thanks for the info."

"Try to keep your girlfriend out of this, will you? MacKinnon's already on edge. Best not to poke the bear."

"Noted," Walker said and then he ended the call. He did a couple of stretches while he thought about what Suzie had said. As far as he could tell, nothing official was going to happen unless the unfortunate Paul Gunn either died or woke up. But that still left the missing evidence. If a cop was involved – and if he believed Alice then he didn't see any other solution – then Walker hated the idea of them walking about with no repercussions. And who was to say that they weren't jeopardising other criminal investigations right at that moment?

Walker continued his run at a slower pace back to his flat. His mind was on Alice and the problems with the case. He let himself in and was glad that he only had to go up one flight of stairs. The run had helped clear his head, but his legs felt heavy and the hangover was threatening to return. When he got to his floor he stopped.

A large figure was standing in front of his door.

"Who are...? Ru, is that you?"

His brother Rhuraidh grinned. "Hi Owen, I've come to visit!"

It was only then that Walker noticed the suitcase next to the door.

"Bloody hell, you don't like to give a guy a warning, do you," Walker said, laughing. He pulled his brother into a quick hug. Ru had always been taller annoyingly, but he had filled out recently so that it was like hugging a mountain.

"Let's get you inside then," Walker said, opening up the door. "What are you doing over in Invergryff?"

Ru had been living just over the border in Carlisle for years. In all honesty, the difference in location suited Walker perfectly well. Since they were kids, they hadn't exactly got on. They used to drive their parents mad with their fighting. As adults they got on much better if they exchanged Christmas cards once a year rather than spending any meaningful time together.

"I'll be honest, Violet has kicked me out."

"What did you do?"

Ru frowned. "You assume that it's my fault?"

Walker said nothing, merely waited. Eventually, his brother laughed.

"Okay, it was totally my fault. I was sending some texts to a girl at work. Nothing too bad, honest, and we never did anything in real life. But Violet saw the texts and well… that was that."

Nothing new there then, Walker thought. His brother was one of those guys that couldn't help but respond to any sort of attention. He was an overgrown child in that way, but there was no point in being annoyed with him. A shame, though. Walker had only met Violet once, but she had seemed perfectly nice.

"How long do you think you'll be staying," Walker said, trying not to sound too unwelcoming.

"Couple of weeks if that's okay? I need to sort out a flat."

"Of course. No problem. What about your work?"

"I've brought the laptop. They said I could work from home until I got my circumstances sorted. My boss has been married three times so he knows the score."

Ru had some sort of job in IT that seemed to make him oodles of money for not very much effort. Walker had always envied the cash, while knowing that that sort of work would bore him to tears.

"I'm dying to meet this girlfriend of yours while I'm here," Ru said. "The one with all the sprogs."

Walker felt his stomach clench. He had no desire whatsoever to expose Mary Plunkett to his brother. Or any of his family, for that matter.

"I'm sure we can arrange something," Walker lied.

"Great. Got anything to eat lying around? I'm starving."

Walker went into the kitchen and opened the fridge. Like most shift workers, he wasn't the best at having fresh food in. He tried the freezer and found a pizza hidden away on one of the shelves.

"Pizza do?"

"Sure. I'll take you out for dinner if you like? There's got to be somewhere in Invergryff that isn't too terrible, right?"

"Aye, there's a few places," Walker said, feeling the slight as if it was directed at himself. "Not like the metropolis of Carlisle."

"Fair point," Ru laughed. "We normally go up to Edinburgh to get somewhere decent. Or there are some decent spots in the Lake District. I'm thinking about moving back up here though."

"Really?"

"Yeah. Why not? Nothing to keep me down south now is

there."

Walker didn't say anything. It wasn't like Ru generally followed through on his plans anyway. No point in worrying about something that might never happen.

"I might not be able to manage dinner," Walker said while the pizza cooked. "I've got some work stuff I need to take care of."

"Still loving being a copper then?"

"Yep," Walker said. His brother had ribbed him mercilessly when he had joined up. For some reason shooting people in the army met with Ru's approval, but helping them in his police uniform didn't.

"I'm happy to hang out here," Ru said, stretching out on the sofa. "If you've got a couple of beers to go with that pizza I'll be grand. You won't even notice I'm here."

I'm not sure that's true, Walker thought. In fact, he didn't need to be a police officer to know that his brother was about as close to the truth as your average petty criminal. Except the criminals were a bit more self-aware.

Chapter 13: Bernie

Bernie had been doing some research. It turned out that the reason soap opera star Rochelle Mitchell was in Invergryff was because she was in rehearsals for the upcoming pantomime season. So it seemed worth a quick trip to the newly refurbished Invergryff town hall to see if Rochelle was available for a little chat.

The town hall had had an eye-watering sum of money spent on it, and as far as Bernie could see most of it had gone on velvet curtains. She had to admit though, it did look rather grand.

"Can I help you?" A woman with a clipboard asked as Bernie walked into the main auditorium.

"I'm here to check out the accessibility for the new show," Bernie said, using one of her favourite lies. "Hearing loops, wheelchair access, that sort of thing."

As usual, panic crossed the woman's face. "Ah. Well, I'm sure we've got all that sorted. Um, you should probably speak to Jasmine. She's the producer."

"Great. I'll just take a look around, then I'll go speak to her," Bernie said, with no intention of doing any such thing.

There were a few people milling around in the audience, but being a rehearsal most of the crowd were up on the stage. Bernie made her way towards it, being sure to write the occasional scribble down in her notebook just in case the girl with the clipboard was watching her.

On stage they seemed to be doing a musical number. To Bernie's ears they sounded dreadful, but maybe it was early days. Pantos were one of the few things at the theatre that Bernie actually enjoyed. It was always fun to hiss at a villain, she felt, although she often found the plucky heroes rather disappointing.

"I can't believe you don't know the words yet," a familiar voice called out from the stage. Rochelle had her hands on her hips and she was glaring at a young man in what looked like a lion costume.

"I know them fine, you just missed your cue," the man said, fixing his tail which had come loose.

Rochelle looked about to take it further, when a stressed-looking older man with gold-rimmed glasses told them to "take a break". Bernie was sure that as Rochelle stormed off the stage she muttered the word "amateurs".

Living up to her diva reputation, Bernie noted with glee. There was something so lovely when celebrities were as dreadful as you imagined they would be. She made sure she saw which way Rochelle went and slipped out of the auditorium to follow her.

The refurb on the town hall was so new that Bernie had to breathe through her mouth to avoid the smell of fresh gloss paint. She hurried after Rochelle who disappeared into one of the rooms in the newer part of the building. Bernie waited a few minutes, then knocked on the door which she noticed was the only one with a name cellotaped onto the paintwork.

"Who are you?" Rochelle was already out of her costume and into a knitted dress that was probably a full size too small.

Something about the woman told Bernie to be honest. "My name is Bernie Paterson and I'm a private detective. I'm investigating what happened to Paul Gunn on Sunday."

Rochelle's lipsticked mouth hung open. "A detective? Really? Well, I have to say it's about time. I tried talking to those police officers, but they only took a statement and then never called me back. I had so much more to tell them?"

Bernie allowed herself a smug smile. She had judged correctly that Rochelle would enjoy being the centre of attention.

"That's why I came to speak to you," Bernie said. "I heard that you were the person that knew the most about what really happened."

"I was right next to him. I had just been helping him smash his nuts."

"Sorry?"

"For the brownies. Honestly, the whole thing was a disaster already. They'd told me it was going to be shown as a special on the local telly station, but then that director Josh, said he didn't know if it would go out at all. Bloody waste of my time. I didn't even get to sing."

"You were going to sing? On a baking show?"

91

Rochelle nodded. "My new Christmas single. They said it could close out the show, but of course that didn't happen, did it?"

"Had you met any of the celebrities before?" Bernie asked.

"Only Paul. We'd both been on that Hogmanay show, you know, the one on the BBC that they film in September. We hit it off. He was such a sweetheart. I can't believe that someone tried to kill him."

"You think he was attacked, then?"

"Of course! He was drinking this cup of tea, and he said it tasted a bit funny. Then a minute later he was unconscious!"

Rochelle's voice got squeakier when she was agitated. Bernie could hear the exclamation marks and it was giving her a headache.

"Why would anyone want to attack him?"

The other woman shrugged, something that caused a wave effect through the exposed flesh that made Bernie want to offer her a coat. "Envy? You get a lot of jealousy in this game, and Paul was doing well. That's why I'm so annoyed about it all. We were planning on doing a project together, a six-episode primetime show looking at our family backgrounds."

"Your families?"

"Yeah, we both come from complicated family histories. Paul never knew his dad and my dad died when I was six. So we cooked up this idea about showing how successful you can be from a broken home. That sort of thing. Paul was well up for it, but it'll have to be shelved now. Unless he makes a full recovery. Could make a great final episode."

Bernie must have shown distaste as Rochelle gave her a filthy look.

"You think I'm a money grabber or something? That I should be crying my eyes out instead? Well, I'll tell you something for nothing, Paul Gunn wouldn't have been bothered either. We've both been around the block a few times and we know the score. You work, or people forget about you, and then you might as well be dead."

"So you weren't interested in Gunn for anything other than career reasons," Bernie said, reckoning that if Rochelle was already mad at her she might as well ask the sleazy questions.

Instead, the woman barked out a laugh. "I don't think so. I'm seeing a dancer off *Strictly* at the moment, older guys aren't really my scene. Mind you, if the papers want to print a picture of me next to Paul looking sad, I'll let them. Gotta sell a few more copies of the single."

"Singing and telly and panto? You must be busy."

"It's all about working on a portfolio. What, you think because I'm an actress I'm thick? I've got an MBA in business. I know that my career has a shelf-life and I'm determined to get as much money as possible before they decide I'm too old to be on the telly. Nothing wrong with that is there?"

"No," Bernie said. She was surprised to find that she felt a

93

moment of admiration for the woman. She was making the most of what she had, and why the hell not?

Bernie left Rochelle with a promise to let her know if anything changed with Paul Gunn's condition. The woman was convinced that he had been poisoned by someone jealous of his success, but Bernie wasn't quite sure that rang true. A has-been star working on local radio didn't seem like the target of that sort of campaign, but she would note it down in the case file anyway.

On the way home Bernie nipped to the shops to pick up some vegetables for a stir fry for dinner. Despite Bernie's best efforts, Finn had never embraced low carb, but she found if she smothered the veg in chilli sauce then her husband would eat just about anything.

Just as Bernie was packing her bags, she bumped into Mary.

"Lauren's pretty miserable," her friend said, shoving her shopping into her pockets. "I've just left my mum with her and nipped out to get some medicine to take down her temperature. This is the first time I've left the house today," Mary said, and sure enough she looked even scattier than normal. Bernie only just resisted the urge to run a comb through the woman's hair.

"I've just been in to see Rochelle Mitchell," Bernie said.

"Ooh, was she as pretty in real life?" Mary asked.

"Nah, wearing a dress size too small might make your boobs look bigger but it doesn't hide the crow's feet around your eyes. There's no way she's as young as her website suggests."

"Interesting," Mary said. "Did she say why she was in visiting Paul Gunn?"

"She gave me some reasons, but I'm not sure if they are true. Apparently they 'hit it off' at the Cook-Off and she was going to appear on his radio show. And do some documentary thing together. I wonder if the old smoothie was trying to chat her up."

"He's married isn't he?"

"Yeah, and I'd really like to chat to the wife. Mind you, even if she has motive, she can't have been the poisoner. It has to be someone at the Cook-Off. Helped along by a friendly police officer to hide the evidence."

"We don't know that for certain," Mary said.

Bernie just snorted to let her know exactly what she thought of that statement. "Seems to me like it's a game of snap."

"How so?"

"We've got two lists. One of the celebrities and staff that had access to the man's cup. The other is the list of police officers who were in the room when it disappeared. All we have to do is find a connection between a person from each list, and there you are. Our killer and accomplice."

"I'm not sure it'll be that easy," Mary warned.

Bernie brushed this aside with a wave of her hand. "Of course it will be. Now we just have to get this list to Liz and she can start going through their financial records. If there's a connection, then she'll find it."

"She's meant to be on maternity leave," Mary reminded her.

"Yeah, so she's got the easy job. You and I will be looking for the other connections. The sort that don't turn up in people's bank accounts. We're going to do some good-old-fashioned interviewing."

"Where do we start?"

"The celebrities. We'll wait for Walker's report on the cops."

Mary nodded. "We'll take them one by one. See if there's any connection with Paul Gunn. But we're going to have to bluff our way in to see them. Like poker."

"Never understood poker," Bernie said. "Too many rules that you're not allowed to break. Much prefer snap."

"I remember you played snap with my kids once," Mary said. "And you cheated so that you beat every one of them."

"Of course," Bernie said happily. "Teaches them a valuable life lesson. Cheaters always win. And that's just how I intend to solve this case before the police. Just you watch me."

"I always do," Mary said and Bernie pretended not to hear the sigh that followed her words.

Chapter 14: Mary

When Mary got back from the shops and sent her mum home, Lauren was still in her pyjamas wrapped up on the sofa. The morning had been a nightmare, running around after everyone with one sick kid. The other children still had to go to school so the little one had been strapped into her car seat under a blanket for drop off.

"Have a lovely day. Make good choices!" Mary had called out to her kids from the window of the car before driving back home. The latter comment was mainly directed at Peter who had been sent home with a note from his teacher requesting him not to use swear words in other languages. Mary had secretly found his knowledge of Japanese quite impressive.

Lauren was watching cartoons on the sofa while Mary put the shopping away. Mary had managed to get her daughter to eat a little buttered toast but that was it. Her temperature had dropped a little with the medicine but had spiked back up. Mary was just thinking about phoning the doctors when her mobile rang.

"Hello?"

"It's me," Bernie said. Mary wasn't surprised, even though she had already spoken to her friend at the shops. With Liz on leave, someone had to be Bernie's sounding board, and Mary didn't mind. Despite the attitude, Bernie generally had something interesting to say.

"I'm heading out to interview some more of our celebrities. Fancy coming?"

"I can't. Lauren's still sick. But do you think…" Mary looked at Lauren who had fallen asleep once more. "I'd love your opinion. Could you pop by here on your way?"

"Sure," Bernie said and then she hung up.

To distract her from staring at her sick kid, Mary switched on her laptop. She had started noting down anything interesting on the social media pages of the Cook-Off celebrities. Each of them had what might be called an 'online presence', but some of them spent more time on social media than others. Paul Gunn, for example, had a website that hadn't been updated in two years and some social media pages which no one had posted anything on for even longer. In comparison, One-shot Sam's entire life seemed to be online from the age of sixteen. In truth, Mary found it terrifying. She was thankful that her sixteen year old mistakes were not online for the world to see.

From what she could gather, Sam seemed to have managed not to post anything particularly stupid, and a quick search online didn't suggest there had been any scandals over relationships or supporting the wrong person, which in itself was surprising. The closest he had come to being 'cancelled' was a post where he had worn a fur coat, only for him to later explain that it was fake fur, set up an online store selling the coats at two hundred quid each and by the looks of things making a tidy profit out of it.

A proper success story, and apart from the Cook-Off, Mary couldn't see any evidence that he and Paul Gunn had ever spent any time together. She put the teenage sensation down at the bottom of the suspect list.

Next she pulled up everything she could find on the newsreader, Nevyn Petty. All his social media seemed to be run by the news channel, and if he had a personal page she couldn't access it. He appeared a few times himself in local newspaper stories, mainly raising money for charities in fun runs and abseils. Mostly for a charity called Huntington's Action. She was just about to look at their website when the doorbell rang.

"Thanks for coming over," Mary said when she opened the door to see Bernie in her usual lycras.

"Is it something to do with Alice? Or the case?"

"Oh no, nothing like that," Mary said, already cringing at the bollocking she was about to receive. "It's Lauren. She's not well and I wasn't sure whether or not to take her to the doctors. I was hoping you might take a wee look at her before you went to interview the suspects."

Bernie sighed. "It couldn't wait?"

"Not really. I know you're going to tell me I'm a worrier, but if you wouldn't mind just taking a wee look at her. She's been off her food all day."

Bernie gave her a sharp nod. "Where is she?"

"On the sofa."

Mary busied herself in the kitchen while Bernie checked out

Lauren.   She was ready for the inevitable 'wet lettuce' comments when her friend returned a minute later.

"All right, you can say it, I'm being ridiculous."

Bernie put her hand on her arm. "We need to take Lauren to A and E. Right now. I think she has meningitis."

Chapter 15: Alice

It wasn't hard to find out where someone lived, and you certainly didn't have to be a Special constable to do it. All you had to do was to go in the staff room and have a root around someone's jacket pockets until you found their wallet. Thankfully, Alice had thought to do just this before her meeting with MacKinnon.

The supermarket next to the new build estate on the west side of Invergryff sold enough baked goods to keep a certain Mrs Plunkett happy. Alice was loitering by the freshly made croissants when a familiar figure walked past.

"Hi, Brooklyn like the bridge," she said, stepping out in front of him.

"Oh hi, Alice, isn't it?" Brooklyn blushed red from his cheeks to his neck.

"That's right," Alice said, offering him a smile. He wasn't quite as young as she had initially thought, Alice realised, probably mid-twenties like her just with a fresh-faced look that made him seem younger. And he was wearing a Dungeons and Dragons t-shirt, which moved him up ten points in her estimation. Not that Alice played herself, but she liked people that weren't afraid to own up to their geekiness. It reminded her of Mary.

"I didn't know you lived around here," Brooklyn said.

"I just came to do some shopping."

"Really? Funny that we should bump into each other when we only just met yesterday." Brooklyn, it turned out was no fool.

"I was hoping to talk to you."

"I don't think –"

"You don't think it's wise? I get it. I just want five minutes of your time. Please."

Brooklyn nodded. "All right. There's a bench in the park just over the road. Meet me there in five?"

Alice couldn't help but roll her eyes. "I'll be the one in the black fedora," she said.

"What?"

"Never mind."

Sure enough, five minutes later Brooklyn sidled over to the bench and sat down. His leg immediately started to jitter and Alice wondered if the man might flee before she started speaking.

"You know why I'm here."

Brooklyn nodded. "You think that someone moved an evidence bag at the event on Sunday."

"Not just moved, removed."

"I didn't take it."

"Did you see who did?" Alice stared at him while he answered, but she didn't see a flicker of guilt cross his face.

"No."

Alice felt her shoulders slump. "And I guess you didn't see it on the table either. God, any longer and I'm going to start thinking I really did imagine the whole bloody thing."

"I did see it on the table," Brooklyn said.

Now it was Alice's turn to stare. "You did?"

"Yes. A large evidence bag with a cup in it."

Before she could think, Alice leaned over and gave him a hug. Brooklyn stiffened in shock.

"Oh god, I'm so sorry! It's just, I didn't think that anyone had seen it." It was Alice's turn to blush red.

"It's fine," the man said, giving her a nervous smile. "I've put it in my report as well, so you don't need to worry about that."

"You're a lifesaver," Alice said. She looked down at her feet and they sat in silence for a few moments. "You didn't happen to notice when the bag disappeared?"

Brooklyn shook his head. "I know it was there when I went to take a statement from the assistant, Charlotte Radford, but that was the last time I saw it. When I was assisting with the evidence collection, I noticed it wasn't there anymore. Of course, at that point I just thought that the sergeant had taken it someplace safe."

"You think O'Connor had it?"

He shuffled his feet, and Alice felt an urge to tell him to sit up straight. He looked more like a child when he slouched. "I didn't see her with it. I just assumed because she was the senior officer that she would have it."

"Right. I wish we had some clue who took it."

"Problem is that the only people there were police officers," Brooklyn said, echoing Alice's own thoughts.

"Yeah. And I'm going to make sure I speak to them all."

He looked up at her from under his eyebrows. "You know you should stay out of it, don't you?"

"Yeah. That's not the WWC way though."

"The what?"

"Never mind. Well, thank you anyway, Brooklyn. You've cheered me up today."

"You can probably call me Larry. Seeing as you've already hugged me."

Alice cringed. "I'm so sorry about that. I'm not usually a hugger."

"It's all right. I sort of liked it."

Larry turned and walked away. Alice stared after him. She had a funny feeling that he might have been flirting with her. And she wasn't completely appalled by the idea. Interesting.

Chapter 16: Walker

Walker had never been so glad to get to work. He had managed to avoid a row with Ru who had already strewn his stuff around the entire flat. How they were going to put up with each other for a whole two weeks, he had no idea. The flat was small, even though it was technically two bedrooms he had had to clear his desk out of the second one just to be able to fold out the spare bed. It was irritating. Walker had been doing quite nicely for the last few years by keeping his entire family at arm's length. The idea that one of them was currently in his home, no doubt snooping through his things made the back of his neck itch.

The office was now his sanctuary. He sat down in front of his laptop and went through his list of actions for the day. He was still writing up reports from the football at the weekend. No less than eight petty offences, but they all needed to be properly logged.

He'd been typing for an hour when Sergeant Suzie O'Connor came over to his desk.

"Fancy coming with me to interview Mrs Gunn?"

Walker grabbed his coat before she could change her mind. "I thought we weren't allowed to question her yet?" he asked as Suzie drove them away from the station.

"I had a word with MacKinnon. I'm not at all happy about this missing evidence. The young Special who lost it didn't seem like an idiot to me. If there's something fishy going on, I want to cover all the bases."

"I agree," Walker said, glad that Suzie was on Alice's side. It also meant that the sergeant was unlikely to be the one who stole the evidence if she was willing to draw attention to it. Or at least that was what he hoped. He didn't want the woman to turn out to be a corrupt copper, mainly because he considered her a friend.

"Her husband is stable," O'Connor continued, "so as long as we don't cause her any distress we should be okay. I want to know if Gunn was taking anything that could have caused his collapse."

"The doctors didn't think he was, did they?"

"No. But we all know that not everyone owns up on what they take to their doctors. The results aren't back yet, but there are all sorts of things that can affect the heart that you might not get on prescription."

"You think he was doing coke?"

Suzie shrugged. "It's just an idea. He's a so-called celebrity, so it's part of the culture, isn't it? And it doesn't have to be coke. Could be anything, but I'd like to hear what the wife thinks about it all."

Walker was still thinking about Gunn and the possibility that he took drugs deliberately when they arrived at the hospital. He might not seem the type, but then Walker knew that addicts weren't all lying in alleyways in big cities. Sometimes they were the most innocuous-looking people, right up until the point where the addiction took over.

O'Connor must have arranged the interview in advance because when they arrived at the hospital she led him to a room in an empty ward where Mrs Emily Gunn was sitting with a young nurse.

Like anyone with a partner who was seriously unwell, Mrs Gunn looked pale and tired. Her expensive tweed coat and matching skirt suit looked crumpled and she was twisting her wedding ring around her finger.

"Sorry to disturb you at this time," O'Connor said once they had introduced themselves. "But we felt that it would be best for your husband if we could try and ascertain exactly what happened on Sunday."

Mrs Gunn shook her head. "I wish I'd been there. But my sister was getting back from holiday and I said I'd pick her up at the airport. I was going to come along to the after-party, but of course that never happened."

"You didn't find out until he was in the hospital?"

"Before then, actually. The Director, Josh Netterby, phoned me. I managed to meet them at the hospital, but he was already unconscious. They're saying... well, they still think there's a good chance that he'll wake up, but then that means there's a chance he won't, isn't there."

"It's best to stay positive," O'Connor said, and the nurse gave the woman's hand a squeeze.

"Was he excited about doing the Cook-Off?" Walker asked.

"Yes. He'd been talking about it for weeks. He loved the radio show, but he really wanted to be back on TV. He was hoping that the Cook-Off might take off and get commissioned as a series. And there was some documentary thing he was planning too."

"So he didn't seem nervous?" Walker asked. "Wasn't worried about anything or anyone?"

"No. Quite the opposite. And there was someone he was dying to meet. He kept saying that too."

"Really? Who was that?"

"I think it was that woman, Rochelle, they were going to do a show together and… No, that's not right. He'd already met her a few times. This other person was someone new. Or maybe I'm just getting mixed up. I don't always listen that well when he talks about his work."

"Did he know any of the others beforehand?"

"He'd met that Nevyn fellow off the news. Didn't like him much."

Walker made a note. "Can I ask why?"

The woman shrugged. "Old grudges. You don't spend four decades in UK broadcasting without developing a few of them."

Suzie leaned forward. "The doctors still aren't sure what

happened to your husband. Whether it was natural or caused by something he ingested."

"I know. They said he could have been poisoned. And I suppose that's why you're here but it's all just so... unlikely. I think it must have been a heart attack after all."

"Was your husband on any medication? Any drugs that might not come up on his official medical record?"

"I wouldn't know, would I?"

O'Connor caught Walker's eye for a second. The woman was being a bit defensive, wasn't she?

"I find that wives often know a lot more than they let on," Suzie said, probing a little more firmly.

"Not me. I know when it's my place to say something and when it isn't. Do you know that we've been married more than thirty years? At the start he was the typical showbiz guy, heading off with every pretty face that chatted him up. But we stuck through all that and he still came back to me. He can't do without me."

She stuck her chin out in determination. "And we certainly haven't stayed together by telling all and sundry about our business."

"Of course not," Suzie stood up. It was clear that Mrs Gunn's tolerance for questions had worn out. They walked back to the squad car in silence.

"Not sure we're any further on," Suzie said once they had

driven back to the station. "But that woman wasn't giving much away. Strange that she would be so defensive. It's not like she's a suspect."

Walker tapped his fingers on the glove compartment. "He couldn't have been poisoned by something he brought from home, could he? Like a water bottle or something? Then she wouldn't have had to be there to poison him."

"It's a possibility, although I didn't get the sense that she wanted him out of the way. I'll get the techs to have a look through the evidence and see if there's anything that could have been tainted. As long as it hasn't been nicked, of course," she said with a frown.

They walked into the station together and Walker went to his computer to type up his notes. Just as he sat down he turned on his phone and saw he had a message from Mary. He had to read it twice before it sunk in. The words 'Lauren' and 'meningitis' seemed to vibrate through the phone. Mary had written that she was doing 'much better', but how bad had she been before if they'd had to rush her to hospital? He grabbed his bag and hurried out of the station.

"Time for a word?" O'Connor said as passed her in the corridor.

"Sorry, family emergency," Walker said without breaking his stride. He didn't want to waste another second. Mary needed him.

Chapter 17: Bernie

Mary was half-asleep, holding her daughter's hand. Lauren was out too, her chest fluttering slightly to show that she was still breathing. She looked so tiny and fragile, but the colour had already started to return to her cheeks.

"I'm going to nip out for a few minutes," Bernie told her. Mary just nodded. The woman looked three shades paler than she had earlier that day.

Poor Lauren. Bernie had kept a calm face so as not to alarm her friend, but she had been really worried about the little girl. The doctors had already started treatment, and although there might be some setbacks, Bernie was confident that the wee thing would be fine in the end.

So it was time to turn her mind to other matters. It wouldn't hurt just to find out where Paul Gunn's room was, Bernie thought. It wasn't like she was planning on doing anything with the information. In fact, as she was in the hospital anyway it would be a poor show if she didn't at least exercise some of her investigative skills.

She walked towards the main reception first of all, but one quick look at the throngs of patients and visitors told her that it was far too busy. Better to find a quieter spot where there were fewer witnesses. She strolled past the shop and the sad little playthings for poorly kids and found the waiting room for the audiology department.

This was more like it. There was only one old woman there and she was snoozing on a seat, her mouth open and making the occasional snoring sound.

At the entrance to the ward was a small reception desk where a bored-looking woman sat behind a computer monitor.

Gotcha, Bernie thought, walking up to the desk.

"Is it all right if I grab a seat?" she asked the young woman with highly defined eyebrows.

"Of course. Can I help you?"

"Oh no, I'm just here to wait for a meeting with one of the consultants."

The woman frowned. "I don't have any meetings scheduled."

Bernie gave her a smile. "It's in half an hour. I just wanted a quiet minute to prepare. I'm getting ready for an employment tribunal."

"Really?"

"Yeah. Some arsehole tried to grab my bum in the OR. And now I'm the one in trouble, can you believe it?"

"No!"

"Aye. Of course, it might have something to do with the fact that I slapped his silly face in front of a whole team of junior doctors."

The other woman giggled. "God, what a story."

I know, Bernie thought, sometimes I don't know how I come up with them.

"Your name isn't Annie, is it?" Bernie asked.

"Yes it is," the woman with Annie on her nametag said. "Why?"

"Oh, when I was coming along the corridor there was someone looking for you." Bernie was a nurse and she understood what kept all nurses ticking. "It was that Tracey. She was saying that there's a fresh cuppa for you in the staff room."

"Tracey? There's no Tracey here."

"Oh, sorry. Maybe it was Jane?"

"Are you thinking of Joanne?"

"Yeah, that's it. She said there was a tea waiting for you. And a doughnut."

"Okay," the woman said, getting up as if a rope were pulling her towards the promised beverage.

Bernie felt a little guilty that there would be no tea for the woman, but at least she had a chance to check the computer before she got back. She turned it around to face her and thanked her lucky stars that the woman hadn't thought to log out.

After checking that no one was coming, she typed in the name Paul Gunn. It took her a few moments to work out just which

Paul Gunn she was after, but she eventually managed to get a room number for him. She scribbled it down on a piece of paper and hurried away before the unfortunate tea-less woman returned.

Bernie checked her watch. She'd only been gone for fifteen minutes. She didn't want to leave Mary for too long, but it couldn't hurt to just take a peek at Paul Gunn's ward. It was part of the intensive care section of the hospital, just off in a side ward where they put patients that were 'stable' but not getting any better.

If only I'd thought to bring my uniform, Bernie thought. Her care home tunic wouldn't pass muster amongst the hospital employees, but it might just have fooled the young police officer who was sitting in the corridor dozing on a plastic chair.

First, Bernie walked past him, making sure that she had the right room. There was no window on the side of the ward for her to peek into. There was a circular porthole on the door, but someone had drawn the curtains across it. Very inconsiderate.

She walked back past, hoping there might be a way to distract the copper. Unfortunately, he had opened his eyes and was watching her.

"Can I help you?"

"No thanks," Bernie said, upping her pace.

"Do you work here?" The police officer asked.

"No. You've got crumbs on your shirt, by the way," Bernie

pointed out. This did not seem to improve the man's attitude.

"This is a police restricted area. How about you tell me what you're doing here?"

"Sorry, I was looking for a vending machine," Bernie flashed a crocodile smile. "I thought there was one up here."

The man sighed. "It's around the corner. Just past the nurse's desk."

"Right, so it is. Do you know, I thought you might know where it was? Thanks so much." Bernie hurried away before the man could say anything else. She visited the vending machine, then managed to find her way back to Lauren's ward without getting lost once. A hospital miracle.

"You brought me a chocolate bar," Mary said, the astonishment plain on her face.

"Special circumstances," Bernie said. "You need to keep your blood sugar up."

"I don't know what I'd do without you," Mary said.

"Wet lettuce," Bernie replied, hugging her friend so that she couldn't see her face, which may have been leaking just a little.

Chapter 18: Mary

The smell of hospitals. Was there anything worse? Mary picked at a loose thread on the corner of her cardigan. The doctors had taken Lauren away for a lumbar puncture. When they had said those words Mary had almost broken down completely. It sounded like such an act of violence to perform on a tiny little girl.

If it hadn't been for Bernie, things would have been a hundred times worse. When they'd first rushed into A and E, she had translated any of the Doctor-speak that Mary didn't understand. When Bernie had first said the word 'meningitis' it was like Mary's whole world had stopped turning. The fear that had settled into her stomach had eased a little since they had started treatment, but it was still there, lurking under the surface.

Lauren had cried when they had inserted the needle for the IV drip, but within an hour her colour was looking better and her eyes had started to lose the glassy quality they had had back at home.

"It's me, mummy!" Mary looked up to see Lauren was being wheeled back into the room. Her eyes were red-rimmed, but she looked more herself.

"The lumbar puncture went fine," a nurse said, fussing with the pillows until they were in the right position. "We'll get the results soon. She should rest now."

Thankfully, Lauren's eyes were already drooping. Mary took the moment of quiet to check her phone. They had been at the hospital for a little over four hours. She texted another quick update to her mother who had come over to watch the other kids and was probably going out of her mind with worry. Being calm in a crisis was not one of Nel's strengths.

"Have you told Walker?" Bernie asked, walking back into the room.

A flash of her boyfriend's steady, reliable face entered Mary's mind. "I've sent him a message. But he's on shift so he won't get it yet. I could call the station but... I'd rather wait until we know the score. Matt's on his way from Aberdeen."

Bernie sniffed. Her thoughts on Mary's ex-husband were well-known, but at least she had decided that this was not the moment to voice them.

Mary felt another wave of exhaustion wash over her.

"You know she's going to be fine, right?" Bernie said, looking down at the little girl. "They've got her in for treatment nice and early. And it's most likely viral, so she'll make a full recovery."

Mary's hand shook as she squeezed Bernie's arm. "Because of you. Honestly, if you hadn't got me to take her to hospital, I don't know what might have happened."

Bernie shrugged her off. "I'm just glad I was there."

"Me too."

There was a knock at the door and Matt walked in, face flushed red and out of breath.

"Is she okay?"

Mary gave her ex-husband a hug, and for once it didn't feel at all weird. "She's going to be. They've given her antibiotics, just in case it's bacterial, but they're pretty sure it's viral. We should get the results from the lumbar puncture soon. They've been giving her fluids and her temperature has already started to drop. The doctor said if it's viral she should be out in a day or two."

Matt cuddled his daughter. She seemed happy to see him, but didn't say much before she drifted back to sleep again.

"You must have driven fast," Mary said once everyone had settled down.

"Too fast probably. Might have a couple of fines heading my way. I just wanted to see her face, you know?"

"I know."

"Stephanie would like to see her too. She's just outside. They wouldn't let any more visitors in."

Mary only paused for a second. Of course Matt's girlfriend would have come with him. It was hardly a surprise.

"All right. I should... Well, me and Bernie will get out of your way for a few minutes. You're only meant to have two people at a time anyway."

118

Matt had settled into the chair, his hand holding Lauren's. "Great."

The last thing she wanted to do was to leave that room, but Mary forced herself to follow Bernie out into the corridor.

In the waiting room, Mary spotted Stephanie immediately. They had met face-to-face a number of times, and Mary was always reminded of the cliché of the younger, more attractive second wife. Not that they were married yet, of course. But still. Stephanie did yoga, was an 'ethical vegan' and seemed to spend half her time at the gym. Mary didn't even own a pair of trainers.

Tired and grumpy, she forced herself to put on a fake smile for the woman.

"Hello Stephanie," she said.

"Hi Mary, what a nightmare this is!" Stephanie stepped forward as if about to give her a hug, but then dropped her arms and they looked at each other awkwardly.

"She's doing okay," Mary said, filling the silence. "We're hoping it's viral and she'll be on the mend soon."

"I brought this for her." Stephanie held up a soft white teddy. "She liked to sleep with it at our house."

"Oh." Mary hadn't brought anything. Everything had happened so quickly, she hadn't had a chance.

"That's very kind of you," she managed to say. "Lauren will love it."

119

"Great."

There was another awkward pause.

"Was she very… upset?" Stephanie asked, her young face pale. "She's so little."

Mary took in a deep breath. "She didn't really understand what was happening. But she's doing much better now. Thank you for coming. Really. I know she'll be glad to see you."

A smile swept across Stephanie's face. "Thanks. And I brought her some chia bites. For when she's feeling better. Vegan protein, that's what she needs."

"Mmn," Mary said, her new-found warmth for the woman diminishing a tiny bit. "Let's just see about getting her home first, right?"

"Right. Well, if it's okay I'd like to go in to see her?"

"Of course. We'll see you in a few minutes."

Bernie waited until the door had shut behind her. "Maybe I could ask her about her yoga routine. Did you see the calves on the woman?"

"Not really," Mary said. She was saved from saying anything more by her phone ringing. "Sorry, better take this." She took a few steps along the corridor. "Hello?"

"I just got your message," Walker said. She could hear the worry in his voice. "How's Lauren doing?"

Mary leaned back against the wall and closed her eyes. "Better,

I think. Not all the test results are back, but she's responding to the IV. Meningitis! I couldn't believe it. Do you know if it hadn't been for Bernie, I probably would have shrugged it off as the cold? She didn't have a rash or anything."

"Thank god for Bernie," Walker said, then he let out a sharp laugh. "I never thought I'd say that."

"Me neither, but she's been a bloody saint."

Mary looked over just as Bernie nicked a newspaper out of the hands of a sleeping man in a wheelchair.

"Well, maybe saints a bit much. But she's something, anyway."

Walker laughed. "Aye, she is that."

Chapter 19: Alice

Alice was fuming. She had just turned up for her shift to be told she wasn't needed.

"But I'm on the rota," she'd told the sergeant at the desk.

"Aye, but they've asked you to stay home for today. Because of that business at the Cook-Off. You were meant to get a call."

"Was I now?"

To be fair to him, the sergeant looked embarrassed. "Look, it's not an official suspension or anything, they just want you out of the way so you don't get into any trouble."

"Good to know," Alice said, forcing herself to pick up her bag and walk out of the door before she said anything she would regret.

She walked out of the station and got back into her car. She took a few deep breaths. There was no blood relation between her and Auntie Bernie – the woman was married to her uncle – but sometimes it was like she could feel the Bernie rage boiling up inside her. There was nothing she wanted more than to go and see her bosses and tell them exactly why they were being such short-sighted dumb-asses.

Thankfully, she had enough self-control to drive away from the station. But that didn't mean she wasn't still angry. It just meant that she was going to use her anger productively. She was going to solve the case, no matter what the people back at the station thought of her. And when she presented them with the suspect, they would have to apologise. Maybe.

If she had been Mary Plunkett she would have gone for a big slice of cake, but Alice wasn't a sugar fiend like her friend. Instead, she turned the radio onto her favourite dance station and turned the volume up as high as it would go.

She was just about to pull out of the car park when a shadowy figure tapped on the window. Alice nearly jumped out of her skin, but then she realised it was Sergeant Walker. He came around and sat in the passenger seat.

"Any news on Lauren?" Alice asked. Bernie had called her to let her know about the hospital visit.

"Much better, thank god," Walker said, and Alice could see he was shaken up. "Mary's ex is at the hospital, so... well, I'm trying to keep busy, know what I mean?"

Alice felt that she didn't know the man well enough to unpack the hidden depths of that sentence so she just nodded and kept quiet.

"I've been looking into this Paul Gunn case. I've found a few things out and I was thinking we could go for a drive," he said, looking anxiously around him. "The lab results have just come in and I want to talk to you about them, but not here."

"All right," Alice said, pulling out onto the main street. "We could go to that drive-through coffee place near the gym."

"Perfect. I'll even pay for the coffees," Walker said with a smile. Alice could see why Mary was completely besotted with the man. He was just charming enough not to seem cocky, which was a rare trait in men in her experience.

It took ten minutes to drive over to the coffee place. Alice was dying to ask about the lab results, but Walker seemed to have a lot on his mind, so she didn't push it. Once they both had a cup of tongue-numbing caffeine, he started to speak.

"It took them ages to work out what was in his blood. Mainly because they didn't know what to look for. Eventually, they found out two significant factors. One," at this point Walker held up a finger, "he had a hell of a lot of benzodiazepine in his system. It's mainly used for depression and for insomnia, but according to his medical notes he shouldn't have been on anything like that. And two," another finger went up, "his blood alcohol was 0.18. That's significantly over the limit for driving, and for most people would be showing some effects."

Alice tried to take all this in. "Nobody mentioned that he seemed drunk."

"Could be a functioning alcoholic," Walker said. "You'd be amazed at how sober they can seem at those sort of levels."

"What about the benzos, though? Do you think that means he was poisoned?"

"Unless he did it himself. Accidental overdose is a possibility. But his wife is adamant that he wasn't taking anything, so poisoning could be plausible. Not that they're saying that officially."

124

Alice clapped her hands together. "That's it then. It was a deliberate poisoning."

Walker held up a hand. "Or accidental. We can't make assumptions yet."

"I know what the evidence is telling me. Or would be, if it hadn't been nicked from under my nose. I guess they're taking the missing cup a bit more seriously now."

He nodded. "You can expect a formal interview about it sometime soon. MacKinnon is having kittens, as you would imagine. They've gone back through the rest of the physical evidence to test for benzos, but it's more in hope than in expectation."

"And Paul Gunn is still unconscious."

"Yeah. They're using the word 'coma' now, so that can't be good. Everyone at the station is starting to accept that this might be a murder case."

"If only they had taken it seriously from the start," Alice said bitterly.

Walker just shrugged. "They went into arse-covering mode. It's not surprising."

"Yeah, but they were willing to sacrifice me to do it. That's not something that I'm just going to let go."

It was Walker's turn to sit in silence. Alice knew that the man couldn't understand her position, even if he wanted to. He was a full-time officer, and he had so much more protection than she did. It was only this week that she had realised just how vulnerable she was. And Alice did not enjoy vulnerability. It just made her mad.

"Would you mind dropping me back at the station so I can get my car?" Walker said. "I'm going to drive over to the hospital. Even if I'm not allowed in I want to be nearby."

"Sure." Alice was dying to ask more questions about Paul Gunn, but it didn't feel like the right time. The man was clearly worried sick. Poor little Lauren. Alice had got to know Mary quite well over the last year, and she knew what a lovely bunch her kids were. The thought of one of them being sick was just awful.

"Let me know if there's anything I can do," Alice said as Walker got out of the car.

"Thanks."

Alice sat back and shut her eyes. She felt helpless, both with poor Lauren and the situation at work. But at least she had a little more information on Paul Gunn. It was just a case of working out what to do with it. She took out her phone and dialled a number. Time to take action.

Chapter 20: Walker

Walker parked outside the hospital. Well, as close as he could get given the hospital parking which was two streets away. He sat in the car for a few minutes, not quite sure what to do. He was dying to see little Lauren, the girl that fell asleep in his arms every time he read her a story. But would he just be getting in the way, given that her dad was already there?

But the thought of Lauren's tiny little hand in his when they walked to the park got him out of the car and all the way to the children's ward. It didn't take long to locate Mary. She was fighting with a hot drink vending machine.

"Why can't you make a decent cup of tea," Mary said, glaring at the machine. "It's just some leaves and hot water. It's not hard."

Bernie was next to her. "Just give it a kick," the woman said.

"Don't do that," Walker said. "It's not a day for criminal damage."

Mary pulled him into a hug so tightly that it threatened to crack his ribs. "Thank you for coming. It's been so awful, although I think we're over the worst now."

"It turned out to be viral, and a relatively mild case," Bernie told him. "She might even get home tomorrow, although she'll need total rest for a couple of weeks."

"I can't wait to get home. We've not been here a full day and I already hate it," Mary said, rubbing her already pink eyes. "Don't get me wrong, the staff are amazing, but I just want her in her own bed, you know?"

"Do you think I could see her? I mean, not if it'll upset her or anything," Walker said, trying to sound a little more casual than he felt.

"Matt's in with her right now. But maybe in a little bit? Sorry, I'm a bit all over the place at the moment."

"You don't have to apologise for anything. If I'm going to be in the way, I'll head off. Honestly, it's not a problem," he squeezed her hand to show that he meant it. "I just want to make your life easier, not harder today."

Mary managed a tiny smile. "It's always easier with you around. I'd like you to stay, even if you might just be hanging around."

"That's fine by me," he said, wrapping his arms around her for a moment, then letting go.

"I'd like to head off if that's okay," Bernie said. "I only popped in for a quick update anyway. I'll swing by your place and let Nel know the score."

"Thank you," Mary said.

They watched the woman leave, then found a couple of seats near to Lauren's room. Mary slumped down next to him and rested her head on his shoulder.

It only took a few minutes until Mary dropped off to sleep.

128

Walker recognised the symptoms of mental exhaustion: there had been plenty of times when he'd finished a challenging shift and sleep had hit him like a hammer. He got out his phone and checked his messages while Mary slept next to him.

Where the hell are ya? Ru.

Crap. Walker had forgotten about his house guest. He sent a quick message letting his brother know about Lauren. He had just pressed send when Mary shifted a little and woke up.

"I haven't been drooling on you, have I?" Mary asked, tilting her face towards his and opening her eyes a little. He had never seen her look so tired. Walker wished that he could tuck her into bed, but he knew that she wouldn't get any real rest any time soon. The crash would come at some point, he just hoped he would be there to help when it did.

"Not at all. You can sleep longer if you like."

"Better not. I'll give it another five minutes and we can go in and take over from Matt and Stephanie. They'll probably want to grab something to eat. I had a terrible Cornish pasty from the café downstairs. It was drier than Gandhi's flipflop. I couldn't even complain about it or Bernie would have made me eat some of her sugar-free protein bars."

Walker smiled, glad to see her sense of humour was still intact. "You're doing good, you know. You only have to make it through a few more hours, then you can take her home."

"Talk to me about something else," Mary said, sounding a bit more with-it.

"About what?"

"Anything. I need to take my mind off the word 'meningitis'. Tell me how work is going."

"Okay, I guess," Walker said, smoothing a stray hair from her forehead. "I'm still playing it softly softly on the Paul Gunn case. If people make the connection between me and Alice, it won't go well for either of us. And it might be selfish, but I don't want to jeopardise anything. Not while I've still got a chance at plain clothes."

"Did MacKinnon say anything about your request for a transfer?"

"I haven't made it formally yet. The thing is, I'll probably only get one chance at it. But I was hoping he might put me on the training seminars this week, but there's no sign of that happening."

"Sorry," Mary mumbled.

"That's okay, I can wait."

"If you couldn't be a detective, what would that mean?" Mary asked.

"I don't really understand the question."

"Well, would you stay in the police? That is, if they don't let you become a detective?"

Walker frowned at her. "I hadn't considered it."

"I mean, there would be plenty of other options. It's not like

130

you joined at twenty and haven't done anything else. You've got lots of skills that could be used elsewhere. In the private sector, for example."

"You're not... trying to recruit me are you?"

A tiny smile appeared at the corners of her mouth. "Maybe a little. I guess I'm saying that there are other options. I mean, look at how the force is treating Alice. Is that something you want to be part of for the rest of your life?"

"Until retirement, that's the plan. Thing is, I tried other stuff. The army was okay, apart from all the, you know, guns and walking and wet feet. But I really feel I belong in the police force."

"Huh. Okay. I can offer you snogs from your co-worker, terrible wages and the opportunity to break into people's houses when no one's looking."

"Very funny," Walker said, kissing her on the forehead. "And you're joking about the breaking and entering right?"

"Of course," Mary said, turning so that he couldn't read her facial expression. Probably for the best.

Chapter 21: Bernie

Bernie had managed to get back home for a few hours of sleep, but she was still feeling uncharacteristically lacking in energy when she got up on Wednesday morning. She even allowed herself one of her husband's chocolate biscuits with her usual large mug of black coffee.

Alice had called her late last night. Her niece was at the end of her tether with the police. Bernie had not managed to avoid saying 'I told you so', but she had promised Alice that the WWC would support her every step of the way. The Paul Gunn case and the missing evidence was now her number one priority.

After looking after Mary, of course. Finn had done the school run that morning and had promised to pick up Mary's older kids on the way. Mary had sent some photos of the little one looking much brighter this morning and she might even manage home by the end of the day.

Now that she knew that the child was out of danger, Bernie turned her mind back to the poisoning. She couldn't help but feel a little behind the curve. Alice had explained the lab results, but even they didn't seem conclusive. Gunn had both alcohol and anti-depressants in his system, but no one seemed to know if he had taken them himself or not. They needed more information and it was about time Bernie got some herself.

She looked through the list of possible suspects and settled on the director, Josh Netterby. If anything strange had gone on, he would surely have noticed it. And if he told her that he hadn't noticed anything, well maybe he was the poisoner? Either way she would learn something.

Bernie called around the local hotels and it only took ten minutes to find out which one Netterby was staying in.

"The English telly guy, yeah he's here," Bernie's friend Agnetha told her. Bernie made sure she had friends at every hotel in Invergryff. It often came in handy. "Hell of a mess he makes for the maids. Papers all over the place and then he gets annoyed if they move them to clean up. Tsk! We were only meant to have him for two days but he's extended his stay until the weekend."

"Lucky for me," Bernie said. "Think you can get me in to see him?"

"He's in his room just now. I can't just let you up there though," Agnetha said.

"That's all right. I'll think of something."

By the time Bernie had driven over to the hotel at the old water mill, she had gotten her story all planned out. There was no point in pretending to be a cleaner or a journalist or one of the many fake identities that she employed. There was a fair chance that Netterby would recognise the woman that had performed CPR on one of his stars. No, Bernie would go for a much more simple approach. One she often avoided. The truth.

She had phoned in advance and was pleased to find that the Director was sitting in the café area of the hotel waiting for her when she arrived.

"What's all this about you being a private detective," Netterby said, leaping from his seat when he saw her enter the room. "I thought you were a nurse."

"Former nurse, current detective," Bernie said. "Are you going to order me a coffee?"

By the time the waitress arrived with her Americano, Netterby had calmed down a little.

"When you said you were a detective I was worried that you were going to come after the show. I've had some of those bottom feeder journalists sniffing around here. They've only printed that there was a 'medical incident' so far, but you can tell they're looking for something juicier."

"It was weird, how it happened," Bernie said.

Netterby sniffed. His hair which had been styled into a quiff was now falling low over his brow in a greasy curl. "It's a bloody disaster is what it is. Don't get me wrong, I feel bad for the old chap. But his heart attack has completely ruined my show."

"You're all heart."

"It's showbiz. Gunn knew that as much as anyone."

Bernie took a sip of her coffee. "That's what Rochelle said. She said Paul would want the show to go on."

"You spoke to Rochelle? She's a piece of work. Practically begged for the spot on the Cook-Off and then moaned at the producers every day for a month until they agreed to let her do her song. Have you heard it? Cats on a blackboard have more chance of getting a Christmas number one than that one."

"What about the other celebrities? Did any of them know Gunn before the Cook-Off?"

"Not as far as I know. The kid, One-shot Sam, he definitely didn't because I saw him introducing himself to Gunn who didn't have a clue what a 'streamer' was."

Bernie laughed, even though the only reason she knew what it meant was because of Ewan and his weird obsession with watching other people play videogames.

"I heard that the newsreader didn't get on with him," she prompted.

Netterby frowned. "Oh yeah, there was a bit of an atmosphere there. They sort of avoided each other when we were getting ready. But they were both old pros and when the camera was rolling you wouldn't be able to tell."

"The newsreader, Nevyn Petty, I guess he's gone back down south now?"

"Actually he's still in Scotland. He's filming a piece about drug use in Glasgow."

"I don't suppose you know which hotel he's staying in?"

"Now why on earth would I tell you that?" Netterby narrowed

his eyes.

"Because the more you tell me about everyone else, the quicker I will go away and leave you alone."

"He's staying at the Carlton George Square," the Director said quickly. "Or at least he was yesterday. I called him up to see if they needed any bodies on the documentary. I mean, it's not normally my area but since the Cook-Off finished early, I'm cooling my heels up here. But they were fully staffed."

"Or they didn't want a director whose last show had ended in a poisoning."

"That too," Netterby said sadly. "I've had a thumping headache all day and no one wants to take my calls."

"Magnesium."

Netterby blinked. "What?"

"You're probably low in magnesium. Many men your age are. Along with testosterone, but I can't do much about that one. I've got some pumpkin seeds somewhere."

"Of course you have." Netterby stood up. "Anyone ever tell you that you don't know when to stop."

"Often," Bernie said, placing a bag of seeds into the man's hand. "But you know what else doesn't stop? Crime."

"I'm not sure that analogy works," Netterby grumbled.

"Oh, go and eat your seeds like a good boy," Bernie said, already heading out of the door.

136

Chapter 22: Mary

It shouldn't have mattered, but Mary was just the tiniest bit pleased to see that Stephanie's make-up was smudged down her cheeks and there was a tomato soup stain on her blouse. It was sour grapes, of course, because Mary felt like she'd been dragged through a hedge backwards. Her hair certainly looked like it had. And although Bernie had brought her a change of clothes, she felt icky all over from not having had a shower since she'd arrived. But she would do it all again in a heartbeat to see Lauren looking so well and ready to be discharged.

Mary had agreed that Stephanie could drive them home. Despite the obvious awkwardness, the woman had proved to be an asset over the last twenty-four hours. Matt was still Matt, of course, but Mary had to admit he could have chosen a worse partner. If only she would stop trying to get her to sign up for yoga.

"Matt says you're busy with the yoga studio," Mary said, desperately raking through her memory for something to talk to the woman about as they walked through the hospital together.

"It's going great. So many people have really changed their lives through yoga. Have you ever tried it?"

"No. I never got on with leggings."

"You don't have to wear –"

137

"I really don't think it's me, somehow."

There was an awkward pause.

"You wouldn't believe the hotel breakfast this morning," Stephanie said, trying to fill the silence as they walked towards reception with the bags. "They had run out of vegetarian sausages, so I had eggs and cold beans. It was grim."

"When I was a student, I used to eat cold beans out of the tin," Mary said. "I still steal a couple when I'm making them for the kids."

"The kids eat beans? Peter told me that they were allergic last time they were staying at our place."

Mary snorted a laugh. "Ah, Peter has many allergies, all entirely fictional. Last week he told me he was allergic to homework, mice and getting up before eight in the morning."

"I can understand the morning thing, but where did mice come from?"

"Oh, I found one in the kitchen. I bought one of those humane traps, but then I felt bad that it might get cold, so I just let it out again. It's made a nest under the cupboards somewhere in an old crisp packet. We've called it Beelzebub. I forget why."

Stephanie's face had changed to one of horror. "You're joking, right?"

"Yeah, of course," Mary said, crossing her fingers behind her back. "Sorry, I'm a bit tired so I'm not thinking straight."

"No problem," Stephanie replied.

Mary noticed that there was a bit of a commotion at the end of the corridor. Several nurses were jogging over to see what was happening.

"I hope it's nothing bad," Stephanie said.

Mary was just about to add that seeing as they were in a hospital, it probably was, when one of the receptionists said: "It's good news actually, some guy has just woken up from a coma."

There can't be that many patients in a coma in Invergryff hospital, Mary thought. She took out her phone and texted Bernie to say that there was a chance that Paul Gunn had woken up.

They made their way out to the car park where Stephanie had somehow managed to get a space opposite reception. Mary was seriously beginning to think the woman might have actual magical powers.

Stephanie's car was a sleek, pristine white thing that looked like it had come right off the showroom floor. Mary didn't understand how she did it.

"Is this a new car?" Mary asked as she wrangled a car seat into the back seat.

"No, I got it two years ago. It's a hybrid, you know. Got to think of the environment."

"Uh huh." Mary just hoped that she wasn't leaving scratches

on the chrome as she hauled the seatbelt around the base, trapping her thumb as she did so.

"Damn," she said, sticking her thumb in her mouth. There weren't even any crumbs in the folds of the seat fabric. How the hell did the woman manage it? It did make Mary think that maybe she should have her car valeted. Or at least give it a hoover once a year or so.

"Is that everything in the car?" Stephanie asked.

"I think so," Mary said. "Thanks for giving us a lift home. Bernie took us to the hospital in her car, you see, so mine's back at the house."

"It's not a problem. I know Matt wants to see her home anyway."

At that moment Matt came out of the hospital, Lauren in his arms. Mary felt an unexpected pang of what-might-have-been. Had she done the right thing all that time ago, splitting up her family, letting this newcomer be a stepmother to her children?

Then Lauren reached out for her, and she took her in her arms, burying her head in the child-smell of her hair. And Mary remembered the lies, the endless money problems, and the fact that after Lauren's second birthday she had gone to find the book tokens given to her by her great-grandmother and they had been sold online so that Matt could plough another tenner into his gambling addiction.

Yes, it had definitely been the right decision. But that wasn't to say that it didn't hurt, just a little, every time she saw him.

Mary sat in the back with Lauren while they drove through Invergryff. Her wee girl chattered all the way home, about her medicine, her hospital friends, the new friends she had met there. Mary couldn't believe how much energy Lauren had left, especially as she wanted nothing more than to curl up in the foetal position and sleep for a month.

"You'd think she'd been to Centre Parks, not Invergryff Hospital," Matt said.

"God, do you remember when we went there just after she was born," Mary said. "Johnny got stuck half-way down one of the water flumes. I still don't know how he did it. I had to climb up and get him."

"And then you remembered you were scared to death of heights and I had to come up and get you," Matt said, roaring with laughter.

Mary joined him, then happened to catch Stephanie's expression in the mirror. The woman had hunched in on herself, staring down at the floor. For the first time Mary wondered how it felt to be the new woman, with the ex-wife in the back of the car and all the memories that she shared with Matt. No wonder she was miserable.

"Do you know, I think I might just sign up for a yoga class," Mary said desperately. "I could do with the exercise. Maybe you could recommend someone in Invergryff for me, Stephanie?"

"Of course!" Stephanie perked up immediately. "I know some brilliant practitioners, even in Invergryff. I'll send you a

141

message."

'Even in Invergryff,' Mary thought, telling herself not to get offended and failing. Thankfully just a few minutes later the car pulled up outside her house. The other kids were at her mother's for the moment, to give Lauren a chance to recover without the usual household of screams, fights and on one notable occasion a full spectacle gladiatorial contest with a colosseum of soft toys watching on.

"I'll pop her into her bed," Matt said, carrying Lauren up the stairs.

"Thanks, I'll get the last of the bags."

Stephanie was still sitting in the front seat of the car when Mary went back outside.

"I should get on up the road to Aberdeen," Stephanie said, checking the time on her phone. "Matt's going to stay for a few more days in the hotel, but I've got to get back to work."

"Of course. Yoga doesn't teach itself, does it?" Mary said trying not to be sarcastic even though it sounded that way anyway.

"No."

"Why don't you come in for a cuppa?" Mary asked, even though she knew the woman would say no. It was an unspoken rule that Stephanie stayed in the car when the kids were dropped off, and that had always suited Mary just fine.

"Oh, well, if you don't mind?" Stephanie said, already climbing out of the car and walking up the concrete slabs to the front door.

"Um, no. Not at all," Mary hurried ahead so that the other woman wouldn't see the instant regret on her face.

Showing Stephanie into the living room, Mary really wished that she had had a chance to tidy up. Or at least run a duster over the place. She could see Stephanie's eyes noting every tea stain and squished raisin on the carpet.

"Matt's upstairs with Lauren. I'll just make you a tea, will I?"

"Do you have decaf?"

"I'll just go and check," Mary said, knowing fine well she had no such thing. With four kids, she had never once thought that she needed *less* caffeine. She opened and closed the cupboard doors a couple of times. "Sorry, just normal tea. Or peppermint, if you like?"

"Peppermint would be lovely."

Mary pulled out the dusty box of peppermint tea from the back of the cupboard. She had bought it because peppermint tea always smelled amazing, but never drunk it as soon as she remembered that it tasted like wet grass.

She made the teas then came back to sit with Stephanie.

"It's very cosy in here, isn't it," Stephanie said.

"You mean small," Mary said, brushing off the implied criticism. For one more day, she was determined not to be

143

annoyed by Matt's partner. "And yes, it is a bit cramped. But we like it."

"It must have been a bit of a change from the house in Aberdeen," Stephanie said.

Mary pretended she hadn't heard that one. The five bedroom luxury home in Aberdeen was worlds away from her tiny semi in Invergryff. But that one had been a sham, paid for by debt and threatened by Matt's obsessive gambling. Best not to go into the torrid circumstances of her divorce with the new woman on the scene.

Matt came down the stairs. "That's Lauren all settled in bed."

"Thanks. I'm going to sleep in with her tonight, just to make sure."

Stephanie stood up and Mary noticed she hadn't touched her tea.

"I've booked another couple of nights in the hotel near the airport," Matt said. "Could I come and see her again tomorrow?"

Mary had been hoping to keep Lauren to herself, but she realised now that was just being selfish. "Sure. I mean, she'll need to rest, but I know she'll want to see her dad."

Stephanie made her way to the door, with Matt going to see her off. Mary called out to her. "Thank you. Both of you, really. Um, thanks for all your help, Stephanie. I'm glad you came."

144

She was rewarded with a dazzling smile. "I'm just glad it all worked out okay. We'll have to arrange a weekend with the kids after our holiday."

Stephanie went out to her car. Don't ask him, Mary told herself. It's better not to know. If you ask him you'll regret it.

Matt came back into the room and made himself comfy on the sofa.

"Where are you going on holiday?" she asked, and instantly wanted to smack herself in the mouth.

"Maldives. Got a good deal."

"The Maldives? Wow, it must have been a really good deal," Mary added.

She saw Matt's back stiffen. "It was a last minute offer. And I got a bonus from work. It's not on the credit cards, before you ask."

"I shouldn't have asked you," Mary said. "Force of habit."

"Maybe I should cancel it anyway. Just in case anything happens with Lauren."

Mary shrugged. "I wouldn't. You know if anything changes I'll let you know straight away. The hospital said a couple of weeks of rest and she should be back to herself. Thanks to Bernie they caught it early and she's had the mildest of cases. Apart from a bit of paracetamol to take her temperature down, she's not even to take any medicine. We've been very lucky."

"We are lucky, aren't we?" Matt said.

"Yes," Mary said with a smile. "We are. Now when are you going back to the hotel?"

Chapter 23: Alice

Alice was doing a job for the WWC on Wednesday morning and she was feeling quite pleased about it. Since joining the Specials she had been feeling increasingly guilty about moonlighting for her Aunt's company, but that had changed. If the police were going to treat her like she was the guilty party then she didn't feel that she owed them the slightest bit of loyalty. Her time belonged to the Co-operative, for the moment at least.

And there were worse employers. At least the WWC made sure that there was always tea and biscuits available, and gin and crisps after six p.m. Even if it did mean she had to pretend to like the dreadful slimming food that Bernie favoured.

Alice was learning that a large part of Bernie's skill at being a private investigator seemed to lie in the fact that she knew absolutely everyone in Invergryff. And if she didn't know them then some member of their wildly extended family would.

On Wednesday, Bernie had called to say that her older sister Martha knew someone who knew someone who had heard that some of the crew that had worked on the Cook-Off had been from the media studies department at Invergryff College.

As the youngest-by-far member of the WWC, Alice had found herself volunteered to pretend to be a college student for the day and go and see what she could find out. At least she didn't need a disguise this time, Alice thought as she put on her normal clothes. She had only recently graduated from her photography HNC, so it wasn't hard to blend in.

It didn't take much of an effort to get to know the media students. Alice had already checked the timetable on the website, so she knew where the classroom was and when the break time was. After that she just had to ensure that she was in the right place when the students spilled out into the corridor.

"Hi," Alice said, walking over to a group of half a dozen students. "Are you all doing the media course? I was wondering if you could tell me a bit about it. I'm applying for next year."

Very quickly she was cornered by two young lads who used the opportunity to explain every aspect of the course in tedious detail, while trying inexpertly to flirt with her.

"What about practical stuff," Alice said when she managed to get a word in. "I heard they arrange work experience for you, those sorts of things."

"Sometimes," young lad number one with the freckles said. "Depends on the lecturer."

"I was hoping to get into telly, you see. Maybe have a shot at doing some camera work."

The other lad snorted. "They don't let us do anything that fun. But there's a decent studio set up here. I could show you around if you like?"

Alice decided to side-step that one. "Weren't a lot of you asked to be part of that Cook-Off thing the other day? One of the lecturers mentioned it to me."

"Only a couple of people were picked," Freckles said, clearly he hadn't been one of them. "Freya was working that day, weren't you Freya?"

A girl with fake eyelashes and long straight hair looked up from her phone. "What was that?"

"You were working at that thing where the guy collapsed. The Cook-Off."

"Aye, I was. It wasn't really working though was it," she said with a sniff. "I did a ten hour shift and they said it was 'work experience'. Never got paid a penny for it."

"That's a cheek," Alice said, working her way over to the girl.

"It's not like I can even put it on my CV. They cancelled it after that old creep died."

"I don't think he died, actually," Alice said. Freya just shrugged.

"Wouldn't care if he had. I made him a cuppa and he never even said thank you. Just looked at my boobs when I was talking to him. Total creep."

Alice tried not to look too interested. This was the first time anyone had mentioned that Gunn had been inappropriate with anyone. And then there was the small matter of the cup of tea.

"He asked you to make him a tea, did he?"

"It was coffee actually. And not just for him. I had to make it for the whole lot of them. They said we'd be learning camera skills, all that stuff, but they just had us making tea and tidying up. Total piss take."

"That's shocking," Alice said. "I bet he didn't even drink it."

"Oh he did. I saw him. Right before he collapsed."

"And it was just a normal cup of instant coffee, was it?"

Belatedly, Freya started to catch on. "What do you mean by that?"

"Nothing. It's just… well, there was a rumour going around that he might have been poisoned."

"What is this, are you filming me or something?"

"No. I guess I was just curious about it. But if you said it was just a normal cup of coffee… Do you think someone could have put something in it after you made it?"

"If they did it must have been one of the people on stage, because he brought it right out to the table he was cooking on. But the guy was really, really old, so it was probably just a heart attack or something."

Freya went back to her phone. If she was an attempted murderer then she was playing it impossibly cool. Alice reckoned the girl had done exactly what she said: made the coffee and given it to Gunn. And that meant that their poisoner had to be one of the celebrities.

Chapter 24: Walker

It was only halfway through his shift but Walker was already watching the clock until home time. His brother had decided to stay up late to see him after the hospital and had insisted they get a curry and have some beers. Drinking two nights in a row was not something that Walker's metabolism enjoyed any more.

Despite demanding they sit up together, Ru hadn't been in a talkative mood. Walker got the feeling that despite claiming not to care, he was upset about the breakup. His brother had never been able to be faithful in relationships. It was infuriating to watch. If any pretty girl spoke to him he would never be able to resist taking it further. One of the reasons Walker hadn't spent much time with his brother was that he found the constant need for attention draining. And now Ru was in his flat and Walker would be expected to fawn all over him. Well, he wasn't a kid anymore and he didn't have to put up with that sort of nonsense. Walker decided that he would have a little chat with his brother that night and maybe tell him some home truths.

"Can I bend your ear?" Suzie O'Connor said, arriving at his desk.

"Sure," Walker said. O'Connor pulled over a wheelie chair from another desk and sat down. "I heard you want to join SCD."

"That's right," Walker replied. "I know that you got in pretty quickly, any tips?"

"Work hard and put yourself forward every chance you get. Plus, I've got a degree in psychology so that put me on their radar. You never went to university did you?"

Walker drew a circle on the carpet with the toe of his shoe. "No. I'm not exactly academic."

"Well, that might count against you a bit, but it won't rule you out. Not if you can show them you've got a knack for it. Look, DI Macleod stuck his neck out for me and helped me get into SCD. Maybe I can do the same for you. Want to come along on this Paul Gunn interview with me?"

"I'd love to," Walker said. He felt bad that he hadn't told O'Connor about the Alice connection, but surely it wasn't worth the risk? If he told her that he was helping the Special conduct a private investigation O'Connor would be annoyed at best, and at worst she could alert whoever the corrupt copper was that had stolen the missing evidence. Nice way to justify lying to your friend, Walker's inner voice said, but he did his best to ignore it.

"You can drive us," O'Connor said. "I want to take a look at those medical reports again."

They drove in silence while O'Connor did her paperwork. It felt weird for Walker pulling up to the hospital again. At least this time it was a much less personal visit. He had spoken to Mary earlier and had felt his tension ease when she said that Lauren was back home. She would need a while to recover, but it looked like she had had a lucky escape.

O'Connor led them to the ward where Gunn was staying. He had been moving from intensive care to a cardiac ward, which was a good sign that his condition had progressed. According to the nurses, he was able to speak, but they were warned not to overtax him. Mrs Gunn had left to get some supplies, so a stern-looking nurse sat in with them to make sure they weren't overstepping their boundaries.

"Ten minutes," the Nurse said. "No longer."

O'Connor nodded and they went to stand next to the head of the bed. Gunn looked a lot older than the pictures Walker had seen of him online. His collapse had drained the colour from his cheeks and his beard was straggly and unkempt. He had managed to sit up a little, however, and his blue eyes were alert.

"Police?" He asked, his voice hoarse.

"That's right Mr Gunn," O'Connor said and she introduced the two of them. "We won't stay long but we need to ask you some questions about Sunday."

"I don't remember much," he said and Walker felt his hopes drop. "I remember getting ready in the morning and the rehearsal, but once we get on stage… nothing."

"Do you remember feeling unwell?"

Gunn shook his head. "Not at all. I was looking forward to the Cook-Off."

O'Connor looked down at her notes. "Did the hospital discuss

154

with you the results of your blood tests?"

Gunn's jaw clenched. "I didn't realise that those sorts of things were divulged to the police." Funnily enough, he suddenly sounded a lot more aware than he had a minute ago.

Suzie gave him a disarming smile. "When it is pertaining to a crime then we have to be informed, I'm afraid. And you did say that you thought someone had tampered with your drink."

"I'm not sure. I'm afraid I don't remember that," Gunn coughed and the nurse handed him a glass of water, using a straw so that he could drink it.

"Are we done?" the nurse asked.

"It was benzodiazepine and alcohol that they found in your blood," O'Connor said, no longer smiling. "Would you know anything about that?"

Gunn shuffled in the bed. "I might have had a small drink to steady the nerves before I went on stage. It wasn't like I was driving."

"And the benzos?"

"I have no idea what they are."

Walker and Suzie exchanged a look.

"So you're saying that you definitely didn't take the benzodiazepine."

"No, I did not. I think I need a rest now."

They decided to leave before the nurse could bodily throw them out of the room.

"Do you think Gunn was holding back," Walker asked when they got back to the car.

"I reckon so. His blood alcohol showed that he had more than a 'small drink', that's for sure. And he looked shifty when we asked about the benzos."

"Why wouldn't he just admit it?" Walker said. "They're antidepressants, not heroin."

"To protect his image, maybe? For men of that generation it might still be a big deal to admit to depression."

Walker didn't reply. He wasn't too sure.

"Anyway, I'm going to recommend to the Superintendent that we close down the investigation. I just don't think there's enough evidence of foul play to warrant it continuing."

"And what about the missing evidence bag?" Walker asked.

"That's up to the Superintendent."

Walker couldn't help but feel this was a bit of a cop-out, but he didn't want to say so directly. O'Connor was the detective, after all, and he was just the uniformed cop. But he didn't consider the case closed, and he knew that Alice wouldn't either.

Chapter 25: Bernie

Bernie was just starting to make dinner when the doorbell rang. When she opened the door she had to take a step backwards.

"Oh Christ, who ordered the milk machine?"

"That is an unpleasant thing to say to your friend who has cancelled her maternity leave to help out her frankly unreasonable partner."

Liz was wearing a baby strapped to her front, no wig or fancy extensions, just her natural hair pulled into a haphazard silk wrap on top of her head. There was definitely at least one spit-up stain on her shirt. Bernie wasn't sure she approved of this newer scruffier Liz. She had always admired the woman's dress sense when she was still an accountant. Mind you, it was better than Mary's dreadful penchant for fan clothing. Last week the woman had worn a hoodie with 'Rocking Fraggles since 1983'. Bernie had hinted she might look more professional in some more conventional clothing, but so far it hadn't had any effect.

"Thanks for coming," Bernie said once she had managed to manoeuvre woman and baby onto the sofa with only mild damage to her back. "Give us the little one for a cuddle."

"She's sleeping, you can have a hold later," Liz said. "Now tell me how you've mucked up this case so we can fix it and I can go home and sleep. She was up four times last night and I'm so tired my teeth ache."

"All right." Bernie went over what they had learned so far, particularly the blood results from Paul Gunn. "Well, the problem is that we still don't know if Paul Gunn took the benzos deliberately or if someone slipped them into his drink. He's awake, but we haven't got in to see him yet, so we're still guessing. I would tend to think it was an accidental overdose, if it wasn't for the missing evidence."

"This is the cup that Alice found, right?"

"Right. And I trained that girl myself and there's no way she made a mistake. If she says she put the evidence down safe and sound, then that's what happened. One of those coppers nicked it."

Liz ran her hand over the baby's head as she stirred in her sleep. "Okay. I guess the most important question is why would they take the evidence?"

"To cover up for someone."

"Then there must be a link between one of the police officers and one of the suspects from the Cook-Off."

"That's what I said," Bernie grinned. "It's good to have you back."

"I'm only back for consultation purposes," Liz said, but Bernie could tell she was excited to be working again. Liz wasn't the sort of person to find satisfaction without something outside the house to occupy her brain.

"All right then, here's what I need you to do," Bernie explained. "I need all the records you can find on our coppers. I'm going to get Mary to sweet-talk Walker for their police files, but I want you to see what else you can find. Financial records first of all, if any of them have had sudden windfalls in the last few weeks that would certainly make our job a lot easier."

"It might be tricky, this," Liz said. "I mean, cops are going to know how to conceal their dodgy dealings, aren't they."

"That's why I need my best financial expert to find out all their secrets," Bernie replied.

"All right, I'll get on it. But it'll take a while. You're looking at going on for a dozen people if we're doing the celebs and the cops. I need you to narrow it down for me as much as possible."

"I'm trying but so far I haven't ruled anyone out. Alice spoke to the lassie who made the tea, but she had no connection to Gunn. She gave him the coffee and then someone on stage with him spiked his drink."

"Unless he did it himself."

"But then why would the police cover that up?" Bernie clicked her tongue in frustration. "We're going around in circles on this one. If Paul Gunn overdosed, either on purpose or by accident we don't have a case, so it's better to work on the other assumption."

"And you want to take this case to help out Alice, right?"

159

"Right. At the moment those idiots at the police station would love to make out that she was just careless with the evidence. But I know that's not her style. And even if Alice wasn't involved, if there's a bent copper around I want to know about it."

Bernie's phone began to ring. "Hang on, I need to get this." She listened to the person on the other end for a while, then said, "Thanks, I owe you one," and hung up.

"What was that about?"

"You remember the Dirty Beggar?"

Liz frowned. She hated non-payers almost as much as Bernie did. "How could I forget?"

"I've been working on a little plan for him. Let's just say he's going to be paying up soon enough."

"You haven't been rattling cages again, have you Berns?"

Bernie winked. "Maybe just a little."

The baby made a gurgling sound and opened her eyes. Bernie held her arms out in expectation.

"Fine," Liz said, unwrapping the carrier and passing over the little one. "But if she poos, it's your responsibility."

Chapter 26: Mary

Mary's body clock was completely out of whack. After Matt had gone home to his hotel room, Mary had fallen asleep in Lauren's room on the floor next to her bed. She had awoken two hours later and had a minor heart attack when she realised that her daughter was no longer there. She raced down the stairs to find her in front of the telly eating some dry cereal.

"How are you doing baby?" Mary asked, smoothing the blond curls back from her face.

"Fine. Where's everybody?" Lauren asked.

"Your brothers and your sister are at granny's house for now until you feel a bit better."

Mary waited for her to say that she missed them. Instead, Lauren just looked thoughtful.

"Can I have Vikki's nail polish?" Lauren tilted her head to one side. "And Peter's best car?"

"No," Mary said, pulling her in for a hug. "But you can have a hot chocolate with me and wear your cuddliest dressing gown."

"All right," Lauren said, jamming her thumb in her mouth and turning her eyes back to the telly. Mary couldn't believe how quickly she had bounced back. She barely had a temperature at all now.

Once she had made two hot chocolates – no 'marsmelons' for Lauren, but plenty for Mary who needed the sugar kick – Mary sat down next to Lauren on the sofa. The first thing she did was open up Bernie's case spreadsheet to make sure she was up-to-date with what was happening with the Paul Gunn poisoning case.

Mary was pleased to see that she had been right about Gunn waking up. Not that she knew the man, but having watched him collapse she felt a connection to him. She was surprised that Bernie hadn't managed to wrangle a way into the ward to speak to him yet, but then it had only been a few hours and even her evil genius had its limits.

It was time to do some more social media stalking. One of the best things about working for the WWC was that it legitimised one of the things that Mary had always been good at, and that was finding out other people's secrets. It helped that she was a likeable person. Quite often people simply told her them, whether she wanted to know or not. In these digital times it was even easier. Mary remembered one time when her friend Amy was dating a new guy from Edinburgh. He hadn't had a presence on any social media channels, which Amy found a bit odd, but not totally unusual as the guy was a teacher and said he didn't want his students to find him. It had only taken Mary twenty minutes of searching the profiles of his family members to work out that the real reason he wasn't online was because he already had a wife and kid living happily in Morningside.

She had already checked out Paul Gunn's socials without much result, so now it was time to go a little deeper. He didn't have any children, so that was a bust, but there were his colleagues

162

at the Radio Station and many of them were in their twenties and thirties and had a lot more to look through online.

One particular colleague, a red-headed woman with the mouth-numbing name of Kayleigh-leigh had posted a set of photographs for the previous Christmas night out. There was even a video of them dancing. Mary clicked on it.

Paul Gunn was to the right of the group, only just in camera shot. Mary reckoned he was pretty plastered. He was trying and failing to keep up with the music, his legs shuffling from side to side. And one of his arms was pulled into his chest, trembling slightly. This wasn't a man who had only had one drink. Mary made a note of it. The bloods taken from the hospital had revealed a fair bit of alcohol in his system, and this video certainly confirmed that he liked a drink.

There was a knock at the door.

"Sorry I'm a bit early," Matt said, standing in the doorway. "Do you want me to come back once you've got changed?"

"I am changed," Mary said, standing aside to let him in. "I just put my Grinch dressing gown on over the top."

Matt rolled his eyes, but Mary pretended not to see. One of the best things about being divorced was being able to wear whatever the hell she liked.

"Hi dad," Lauren said, turning around and showing him a big chocolate moustache.

"Hi sweetie," Matt said. "I'm not sure chocolate is a great idea when you're trying to get better," he said with a look at Mary.

163

Keep calm, Mary reminded herself. You only have to survive a couple of days and then he's Stephanie's problem again.

"I've got homemade soup on the stove for lunch and she'll get plenty of fruit and veg for the rest of the day," Mary said, trying to keep her tone light. "A wee bit of hot chocolate won't harm her."

Matt said nothing.

"Did Stephanie get back up the road okay," Mary said, changing the subject.

"Yeah, she's back at work today. She was really worried about Lauren."

Mary blew on her tea. "I know. I hadn't realised how well she got on with the kids, but it was nice to see. You've got a good one there."

"She's pretty amazing really."

Lauren climbed into his lap and hooked her arm under his. "Daddy, can you play ponies with me."

"Sure," Matt said, wincing as he got down onto the floor. "This stuff is bad for my knees."

"Tell me about it," Mary laughed, handing him the tiny brush for the ponies' tails. "Why do you think I've got so many fluffy cushions? I definitely never used to need them when I was twenty-five."

"We went to see the horses with Stephie," Lauren said.

"Did you?"

"There was a race on at the track in Aberdeen," Matt explained. "We took the whole lot of them. They didn't care about the race, of course, but there were some ponies they could pet."

"Horse racing?" Mary couldn't keep her face neutral.

"I didn't have a bet, before you ask."

"I wasn't," Mary said, turning her face away. Don't interfere, she told herself. Whatever you do, don't interfere. And then her inner Bernie burst free. "Matt, it's about Stephanie."

"I know you don't exactly approve. But she has every right to —"

Mary held up her hand to stave off the argument. "I've no problem with Stephanie. I admit it's a bit awkward, but she obviously adores Lauren. And the other kids."

Matt frowned. "Then what's the problem?"

"She's mentioned a few things about the divorce and the house and it made me wonder. You have told her about the gambling, haven't you?"

More than a decade together meant that Mary knew Matt's guilty face instantly.

"Matt! What the hell are you thinking? She needs to know!"

"I'm in recovery. You know I haven't gambled once since you left. And... well, if it's not a problem anymore, then I don't

165

need to tell her, do I?"

Mary bit her lip. She was about to tell Matt exactly how many things were wrong with what he had just said, before she remembered that he wasn't her problem.

"I just… I want you to be happy, Matt. I know people say that, but I mean it. You're the kids' dad and I want things to work out for you. And about Stephanie… Look, you're serious about her. I mean, you're talking about marriage for God's sake. You can't keep this massive lie bubbling under the service. She deserves better than that."

"I know," Matt's bottom lip quivered in just the same way that Peter's did when he was in trouble. "And you're right. I know I'm going to have to tell her. I just have to work out how, that's all."

Was he just telling her what she wanted to hear? Possibly, but Mary knew there was no point in pushing things any further.

"Maybe… I don't suppose you could tell her? You always know the right thing to say to make everything better."

For a moment, Mary was speechless. "No, Matt, I won't tell your new missus your worst secret for you. Jesus, I can't believe you asked."

"You said a bad word, mummy," Lauren said, her face lit up with glee.

"Jesus isn't a bad word," Mary replied. "It's in the nativity."

Matt reached over to Mary as if for a hug, then changed his

mind and patted her arm. "Sorry. I shouldn't have asked that. Life was so much simpler when we were together, wasn't it?"

"Simpler, perhaps," Mary said. "But not easier, Matt. Definitely not easier."

Chapter 27: Alice

Alice was at home, bored out of her skull. Her mother was one of those people who seemed to think that keeping busy was the cure for all ailments. So when Alice had explained the nightmare that was happening with her work, her mother had said – almost gleefully – that there was a full pile of ironing needing doing in the kitchen.

"It'll take your mind off it," her mum said as she turned the telly on to *Strictly*.

"So would playing videogames and eating ice-cream," Alice muttered but her mother just clicked the volume up to eleven.

Stuck for any better ideas, Alice had turned on the iron. At least it gave her a chance to think. Paul Gunn had woken up, and that was a good thing. But the word at the station was that they were closing the case, and as far as Alice was concerned that was very bad. Firstly, because she would never get a chance to clear her name and would always be known as the dozy Special who lost an evidence bag. And secondly because whoever did steal the evidence bag would get away with it. Mary's boyfriend had promised that he would keep investigating, but Alice knew he wouldn't do anything that might harm his chances of making detective. She was on her own.

Except for the WWC, of course. Bernie had laughed when Alice had told her that the police considered the case closed.

"We'll show them," Bernie had said. Alice wished she had her Aunt's confidence. Without the tendency to insult every person she met, of course.

Alice put down the iron. She needed to focus on the missing evidence bag. That was the only thing that mattered now. She had already spoken to Laidlaw and Brooklyn and she knew that Walker had asked O'Connor about it. That just left Kay Morrison. And the thing was, Alice knew exactly where she would be at this time on a Wednesday night. She just didn't want to go.

But it was better than staying home, sulking and ironing her mother's pants. Alice turned off the iron and went upstairs to get changed.

Five minutes later she was in the car driving towards the area of Invergryff that would be described by estate agents as 'up-and-coming' and by everyone else as something that would be unprintable. She parked her car on what she hoped was a half-decent street and made her way to the Craggy Dog.

Alice had been there in uniform before. There wouldn't be a member of the Invergryff constabulary that hadn't. It was prime territory for bar fights, low-level drug deals and what might be called, with geographical accuracy, the Invergryff kiss.

But tonight there would be none of that, because everyone in town knew that Constable Kay Morrison was always at the karaoke on a Wednesday night, and she was tougher than most of the locals. Kay was a reformed troublemaker, a teen that had been a constant irritation to the law before she had seen the light and joined the force herself. It made her a great officer for her community because she had a level of respect that no one else had. Add that to the fact that she had a glare that could freeze your bones, and Morrison was the boss of this part of Invergryff.

It meant that Alice had to force herself to walk through the doors of the pub. A wall of sound hit her. Someone was doing their best Elvis impression on a small stage in the corner of the room and the speakers were turned up to the max. Even though it was mid-week, there wasn't a spare seat in the place. Karaoke in the Craggy Dog was a serious business.

Alice headed to the bar and got herself a soft drink. She let her eyes scan the room until she spotted Morrison, sitting with a group of half a dozen locals at a table near the front.

"Hello," Alice said, moving towards the table. Morrison had a half drunk pint in front of her, and when she recognised Alice she didn't look happy. In fact, severely pissed off would be a better description.

"What are you doing here? Come for a singalong?"

Alice shuffled her feet. "I thought I could grab a word with you."

"Oh you did, did you? Well, you can see there's no spare seats here."

The rest of the men and women at the table looked at them in mild interest. They could tell there was something going on.

"Maybe we could chat outside?"

170

"Not while the singing is on. In fact, why don't you give us a wee number," Morrison grinned the sort of evil smile that Alice had only previously seen on her Auntie's cat.

"I'm not a singer," Alice said, trying to smile.

"It's Invergryff, not the Albert Hall. Go on, give us a song."

"I really don't think –"

"If you want to chat," Morrison growled. "You need to go up there and give me a song."

Alice shuddered. "I really can't sing."

"Everyone says that. Look, I've been told not to go anywhere near you. So if you want me to talk to you then I want to see you up there strutting your stuff. Now stop moaning and get on with it."

Half in a daze, Alice turned and walked over to the man with the karaoke machine.

"Kay says I need to do a song," she said.

"Then you better do one," the man said, scratching his stomach through his polo shirt. "Stevie Fletcher got pneumonia the other week and she still made him get up here and do his 'Yellow Submarine'. I heard they had to give him oxygen afterwards."

"Great," Alice said. "Give me something short."

"How about this?"

Ten seconds later Alice was standing in front of a sceptical crowd, belting out the opening lines to Lizzo's 'Good as Hell'. In hindsight, it was a poor choice. It was only two and a half minutes long, but clearly most of the people in the room had never heard it before. Or Alice was butchering it so badly that they didn't recognise it.

Alice could see the frowns of the people in the audience, who suddenly looked much more muscular and threatening than they had before. I need to play this for laughs, Alice thought, or I'm not going to make it out alive.

Gripping the microphone she started doing the dance routine, which got her a few cheers and laughs, even miming the bit with the flute. It was excruciating, but before she knew it the song was over. She got a small round of applause and no one threw anything at her, so Alice was hopeful that she had passed the test.

Keeping her eyes on the floor from sheer embarrassment she made her way back to Morrison's table.

"That was dreadful," Morrison said. "Don't ever do that again."

"Believe me, I won't."

The woman's face softened slightly. "But I guess you've earned your chat. Let's go out back to the smoking area."

The back door of the pub led to a small courtyard area where someone had erected a plastic marque to keep the rain off and an optimistic sign telling people to dispose of the cigarette

172

ends in the bin.

"You want to talk about the Paul Gunn thing," Morrison said, pulling out a vape pen and puffing smoke into the air. "Even though the case is closed."

Alice shrugged. "I want to talk about the missing evidence. Which for some reason no one seems to be admitting to taking."

"Maybe that's because they didn't," Morrison replied.

"I know what I saw."

"No one's calling you a liar."

There was something in the way Morrison spoke that made Alice narrow her eyes. "Then you do believe me. Did you see what happened?"

"No." There was just the tiniest hesitation.

"You saw who took it?" As soon as Alice voiced the thought she knew it was correct. Morrison didn't meet her gaze.

"Look, this man Gunn clearly doped himself up. There's no case here so I just want you to drop it."

Alice took a step closer to the woman, even though Morrison towered over her. "I could report you for this."

"On what evidence? Can't you just trust me that we're better to forget all of this? Paul Gunn forgot how many pills he took, he's doing fine and he'll be discharged tomorrow. Case closed."

173

"Not for me," Alice said, her jaw clenched.

"Then you can go down in flames for this," Morrison said, already turning to go back into the pub. "But I won't let you take anyone else down with you."

Chapter 28: Walker

Walker had been due to finish at six but there was an outbreak of flu making its way around the station so he had agreed to do overtime until midnight. To his relief, the shift had flown by. After they had interviewed Paul Gunn there had been a sighting of a man wanted all over Scotland for drug trafficking. Someone had grassed him up for dealing out of a pool bar near the station. Walker got to drive 'blue lights' through town, which was always thrilling.

The man, known to his probation officer as Ronnie MacFarland but to everyone else as 'Slasher Ronnie', had been taken in cleanly to the custody suite. There were congratulations all around, especially as a search of the bar had found six figures worth of cocaine and valium secreted in the pool tables.

"Can I have a word, Sergeant," Superintendent MacKinnon had appeared from nowhere.

"Of course, sir," Walker said, springing to his feet and following the man along the corridor. His spidey senses were tingling. There could be no good reason for the Super to want to talk to him at this time of night.

MacKinnon led him into his office and closed the door.

"Good work on the MacFarland bust," MacKinnon said, but he wasn't smiling.

"Thank you," Walker said. He sat in the chair opposite his boss and waited.

"Why didn't you tell me that Alice Paterson was Bernie Paterson's niece?"

Uh oh. "I didn't realise it was relevant, sir."

MacKinnon narrowed his eyes. "You know fine well that it is up to me to decide what's relevant and what isn't. Our Special Constable who is the centre of this whole controversy over the missing evidence is the niece of that... *woman* that calls herself a private detective." MacKinnon had said 'woman' like it was the nastiest of swears.

"They are an official investigative agency," Walker said, finding that for some reason he wanted to defend Bernie.

"That's what makes it worse! This case should already be closed. But if this mess with the evidence gets out, we'll be lucky if we avoid an official inquiry. And now we have these PIs muddying the waters."

"I'm sure Alice doesn't want Bernie getting in the way either," Walker said.

There was a pause.

"You know Alice Paterson well, then?"

Double uh oh. Walker needed to learn to keep his mouth shut. "A little. Through my girlfriend Mary."

"You've not been stepping beyond the boundaries of your job

176

description, have you sergeant? You are developing a bit of a reputation for being unorthodox. If I'm not making myself clear, I do not mean that as a compliment."

"Yes sir," Walker said.

MacKinnon shuffled some papers on his desk. Walker wondered if they were there for effect as the entire force was meant to be going paperless. He still couldn't help craning forward to see if he could spot his name on any of them.

"I know you're looking for a move to SCD. But if you keep stepping over the line it's simply not going to happen for you. You'll be lucky to keep your job at this rate."

"I understand, sir."

"But it's not going to make you change your mind, is it?"

"Probably not, no," Walker said, realising there was no point in lying.

The Superintendent rubbed his eyes. "Do you know, I think you might even make a good detective? At least it would get you out of my station. If you manage to stay out of trouble for a couple of years, I might even put your name forward."

"A couple of years?"

"Let me guess, you were hoping for something quicker?"

Walker nodded.

"Fast track is only available for those that can demonstrate something of value to SCD. Normally that means a degree in a relevant subject. You never went to university, did you?"

"No."

"Then unless you can show SCD some other reason why they might want to recruit you then you're always going to be at the bottom of the pile. And a record of insubordination is not going to help that one little bit, understand?"

"Yes sir."

Walker left the station feeling like he'd had his arse smacked. The thing was, he knew that MacKinnon was doing him a favour. He'd be within his rights to put an official sanction on his record for Walker's involvement with the WWC. He hadn't done that, but he'd made it clear that SCD was a long shot. As Walker drove home he couldn't help feeling sorry for himself. It wasn't his fault that he'd never got on with school. He had always thought he was stupid, and it hadn't been until fairly recently that he had realised that his dyslexia was a big part of that. Maybe if he'd had a diagnosis earlier then he could have gone to Uni, been headhunted for SCD just like Suzie O'Connor.

He arrived at his block of flats and turned off the engine. Or maybe he would have still flunked out. The thing was, he knew that he didn't need a degree to be a good detective. He just needed one chance to prove how bright he was. But MacKinnon had made it clear that he would never get that chance if he kept working with the WWC.

Still pondering what that meant, he climbed the stairs and let himself into the flat. As soon as he saw Ru Walker knew that

178

his brother was spoiling for a fight.

"You're back late," Ru said.

"Work was busy," Walker said.

"Giving people parking tickets and telling them off for racist jokes?"

"Something like that." When Ru was in this sort of mood, it was best just to ignore him.

"Don't know why you stick at that job," Ru said. He was sipping from a beer can and Walker could see another half dozen empties next to the sink. "It's not like it pays you anything."

"I didn't realise I'd asked for your opinion," Walker said, annoyed that the conversation was even taking place.

"Hey, I'm just trying to help," Ru said holding out his hands in apology. "I mean, if you want to support a family of what, five? Six? Then you'll need more than a copper's wage."

"I don't want to talk to you about that," Walker said, looking longingly at the door. "In fact, I don't want to talk to you about anything right now."

"You never do, do you? You always just do whatever the hell you want."

Walker didn't say anything. It wasn't like he disagreed. The whole reason that he had spent the last few years trying to stay as far away from his family as possible was because they never approved of any of his choices.

"Mum was on the phone the other day. She was asking after you."

Walker spat out a laugh. "Here it comes. You know that that subject is off limits."

"But –"

"But nothing. It's time you took a good look at yourself Ru. You've given up on a genuine chance at making a go of it with Violet. And who have you learned that sort of selfish behaviour from? I'll give you three guesses."

"You can't blame our parents for everything."

"I'm not. I'm blaming you for acting just like them. You need to grow up."

"You're one to talk!" Ru's face was growing more and more red, reminding Walker of a ripe tomato. "Look at what you're doing now. Running about after some other man's kids."

Walker felt his breath catch and he had to force his hands out of fists. "Don't go there, Ru."

"Why not? Why should your private life be off limits? Man, that woman must have been over the moon when she got you to take on her baggage."

"You better leave now, Ru, before I teach you a proper lesson. And you know you've never beaten me in a fight."

Ru took a pace towards him. "Aye, but I'm a bit bigger now,

aren't I?"

"Bigger and dumber." Walker stood up. He took a step towards his brother and saw Ru flinch. Did he really think he was going to give him a kicking? "I'm off to bed. I think you should look for a hotel in the morning."

He closed the door behind him before his brother had a chance to say another word.

Chapter 29: Bernie

Bernie always got up early, but on Thursday morning she was up and dressed before six. She had several plans that she needed to put in place and she was humming as she did so, happy that she was about to make a whole bunch of people very angry indeed.

She did an hour on her home spin bike and then checked her stats. Pretty happy with her resting heartbeat and blood pressure she made herself some eggs and a protein shake for breakfast. She was targeting a good time in the half-marathon she would be running at the weekend. Hopefully by then she would have sorted out some remaining WWC business that was preying on her mind.

Paul Gunn was awake and no one was letting her in to see him. This was aggravating her beyond belief. She had tried bribing her friends who were cleaners, her friends who were nurses, even the woman who worked in the hospital shop. But no one had any idea how to get her past the tubby police constable with crumbs on his shirt.

Oh well, at least she was about to clear up one other work niggle. She checked her watch and saw that it was nearly eight. Good, time to get going.

When she was driving into town her mobile rang. She routed it through the car console.

"Hello?"

"It's Agent Emma Peel and I'm in position."

"Agent who?"

"Emma Peel. It's my code name."

Bernie rolled her eyes. "You've not been speaking to Mary, have you?"

The voice at the other end laughed a horse chuckle. "Aye, and she said that all good spies need a code name."

"You're not a bloody spy, you're... never mind." Bernie hung up. She was outside the office anyway, so there wasn't much point in continuing the phone call.

The office of Pierce Mundell, otherwise known as the Dirty Beggar, was on one of the posher streets in Invergryff to the North of the river. Mundell arranged 'financial services' for exclusive clients who would only gain access to the rather swish building if they had an appointment.

Or if they rang the buzzer to say they were the postman, like Bernie did.

By the time she climbed the stairs to the second floor, Bernie could already hear the singing. It seemed to be the warbling sound of the greatest hits of Cliff Richards, in the pre-Shadows era.

"Will you please be quiet," Mundell's secretary said to an elderly lady who was sitting in one of the posh leather armchairs next to reception.

"Hi Bernie," the older woman waved. "I've been here for half an hour already. I even brought my harmonica!"

"You're the one that phoned me, aren't you," the secretary said. She did not look impressed and she had a phone pressed to her ear. "I'm just about to call social services to get this… lady out of here."

"How rude," Mrs Roberta said, clicking her knitting needles together. "Your sign said 'any portfolio size welcome' and I've got two and six in my post office account."

The secretary gave Bernie a dirty look. "I don't know what you're playing at but please just go. Mr Mundell will be here any minute."

"What the hell is that?" As if summoned by his secretary, the Dirty Beggar had just walked through the door.

Bernie tutted. "Mrs Roberta is not a 'that', she is a 'who.'"

"What's she doing in my office?"

"Looks like she's doing her knitting."

Mrs Roberta waved her wool in the air. "I'm sending cardigans to the Ukraine."

"Has anyone warned them?" the Dirty Beggar asked.

"What did he say?"

"Nothing. Poor Mrs Roberta was just looking for a nice warm place to spend a few hours on a chilly day. You wouldn't throw her out in the cold, would you?"

184

"I bloody well would. I suppose I have you to thank for this, Mrs Paterson?"

Bernie shrugged. "I don't know what you mean. I just came to see if you might have that cheque ready for me. Although I have heard that Mrs Roberta does a fabulous Doris Day, complete with dance."

Mrs Roberta jiggled her bosom in a way that made everyone else in the room shudder.

"I will not be blackmailed like this," Mundell said, his face growing red.

"What a nasty word," Bernie said. "All I'm doing is giving you a choice. Not that difficult, is it?"

"I'd decide fast if I was you," Mrs Roberta piped up. "I've had two cups of tea already today and you wouldn't want this to turn into a dirty protest."

Five minutes later, Bernie was back on the pavement with a cheque in her hand and joy in her dark little soul.

"Thanks for your help."

Mrs Roberta let out a giggle that made her seem decades younger. "Thank you for the opportunity to behave so badly. I spent my whole life being a good girl, maybe it's time to be a bit naughty."

What have I created, Bernie thought as she watched the woman hobble along the road, the odd chorus of 'Love me Tender' carrying on the wind.

Her phone pinged to let her know that Alice had emailed her something. Always mindful of the pennies, Bernie nipped into a local coffee shop to order a tap water and take advantage of their free wifi.

She opened up Alice's email. It had a video attachment and a brief message.

The Director sent the unedited footage to me this morning. Check out five minutes in. I'm not sure if it's one hundred per cent clear. You can see Gunn drinking from the mug, but it stops before his collapse. Let me know what you think. Alice.

She downloaded the video, clicking her nails on the table while the café wifi struggled, and then pressed play. The angle was from the right-hand side of the stage and the camera work was a little shaky. It showed Paul Gunn and One-shot Sam walking on stage, mugs in their hands. The rest of the celebrities followed after. They also had mugs, except in the ballet dancer's case where she had a bottle of water.

She watched until five minutes in, then paused the video.

"I can't believe it," she said out loud, then went back thirty seconds and watched again. Then she called Alice.

"Am I seeing what I think I'm seeing," Bernie said as soon as Alice answered the phone.

"You saw it too?"

"Yep. One-shot Sam clearly put something into Paul Gunn's mug."

"That's what I thought."

Bernie whistled through her teeth. "What the hell? The kid did it? But he doesn't even have a motive."

"Or we just haven't found it yet," Alice reminded her.

Chapter 30: Mary

Mary answered her door at lunchtime on Thursday to see a grinning Bernie.

"You look happy," Mary said to the woman as she walked into the house. "Who have you been upsetting?"

"You know me too well," Bernie replied. "Let's put it this way, the Dirty Beggar is not going to be late paying any bills ever again."

Mary let her into the kitchen. "We'll have to be quiet. Lauren's sleeping upstairs. Matt's gone up to check on her and I reckon he's snoozing up there too."

"Great, that means the silly fool won't be interrupting us."

"Ssh, Bernie, what if he hears you?"

Bernie shrugged. "Anyone who's silly enough to throw away a life with one of my WWC members deserves to know all about it."

Mary stared at her. "You're practically bouncing off the walls. You haven't had chocolate, have you?"

"Better than that. After I taught the Dirty Beggar a lesson, I got an email from Alice. Come and see what she sent me."

They sat down on the sofa and Bernie played the clip on her laptop.

"That can't be right," Mary said, rewinding and playing it again. "One-shot Sam? We never even considered him as a suspect."

"Those social media superstars," Bernie tutted. "I always said they had no morals."

Mary leaned back on the sofa. "But I checked out all his stuff online. There's absolutely no connection to Paul Gunn. And why would there be? Why would a streamer have anything to do with an aging radio presenter?"

"We're going to have to find that out. But first, take another look at that clip. If you watch closely you might spot something else."

Mary watched it one more time. Instead of focusing on One-shot Sam, this time she looked at the wider scene. And then she noticed the newsreader.

"What on earth? It looks on here like Nevyn, that guy from the news, was looking right at One-shot Sam when he slipped the pill into the drink. Why didn't he say anything?"

"Why indeed? I reckon we should go and ask him."

Mary chewed her lip. "You don't think we should tell the police about the lad putting something in the drink?"

"The police who said there was no case, is that who you mean? No, I'm not ready for that yet. Besides, I want to find out a bit more about the boy. Make sure we're seeing what we think we're seeing. And I want to ask that Nevyn bloke why he didn't say anything about the drink."

189

"Sounds like a plan."

Bernie stood up. "And I want you to come with me."

"Oh, I don't think I'd better," Mary glanced up at the ceiling, as if she could see through it to her sleeping daughter.

"I know it's hard," Bernie said, "but it would do you good to get out for a couple of hours."

Mary clasped her hands together tightly. "I just don't want to let her out of my sight."

"I understand. But she'll be with her dad. And you've not had a minute without thinking about sickness and hospitals for two days. A few hours out of the house will do you good."

The woman had a point. At that moment Matt came down the stairs.

"Bloody comfy that bed," he said, smoothing down his hair.

Mary looked over at him. "Bernie was asking if I could help her out on a case. Would you mind watching Lauren, just for a bit?"

"Not at all," he said.

"Right. Well, I'd better get ready."

"Definitely time for a shower," Bernie said. "And maybe a bit of make-up."

"Thanks," Mary said, making her way up the stairs. "Put the kettle on Bernie, I'm going to need some caffeine."

190

A shower, a scrub of her blotchy face and a lot of concealer later, Mary felt a bit more able to face the world. She peeked into Lauren's room and saw her daughter fast asleep under her My Little Pony bedspread, clutching her brother's favourite Pokemon teddy. She leaned down to kiss her cheek, then took a deep breath and walked out of the room.

"You look much better," Matt said.

Bernie pulled a rude face behind his back and Mary had to hide a giggle.

"There's food in the fridge and if she needs any medicine it's in the bathroom cupboard."

"Got it," Matt said, flicking on the telly. "Don't you pay for the sports channels?"

"No, I don't," Mary said, dragging Bernie out of the room when saw the look on her face.

"How the hell were you married to him for a decade?" Bernie said as they closed the front door behind them and walked over to the car. "Sports channels indeed."

"I know he's a nightmare, but I only have to put up with it for a few days. It's not worth the row. He's Stephanie's problem now," Mary added, and the thought lifted her heart.

"Fine," Bernie said. "Let's go over our strategy for the newsreader."

"Are we just going to ask him if he saw One-shot Sam put something in the drink?"

Bernie yanked the wheel to one side. "Bloody cyclists. No, I don't think we should ask him straight away. He's a newsreader, he'll be used to difficult interviews. We need to play it a little more subtle."

"Don't take this wrong, but subtlety is not normally your strong point," Mary pointed out.

"I know. That's why you're here."

Mary felt oddly proud.

"And judging from previous scandals, he has a thing for blonds, so that might help too."

"Ah."

The hotel that Nevyn was staying in was a chain-type at the higher end of the market near the airport. When they arrived Bernie went up to the front desk and had a deep discussion with the receptionist. After a few minutes, she gestured to Mary to head to the restaurant.

"He's having lunch," Bernie explained. "The woman at the desk is a second cousin of Finn's and she said we can head right in."

"Is there anyone in Invergryff that you don't know?" Mary asked.

"Nah."

Nevyn was enjoying a glass of red wine with his lunch when Bernie and Mary approached his table.

"Mind if we sit down?" Bernie asked while she pulled over a chair. It made a horrible metallic scraping noise as she pulled it across the floor. Mary made sure to lift her chair and put it down at the table with an apologetic smile.

"We're private investigators," Mary said, taking the lead like they had agreed. "But we're not here to cause you any trouble. We just wanted to talk about Paul Gunn."

"Well, I was just finishing up," Nevyn said giving her a smile full of whitened teeth. "Perhaps I could tempt you two ladies to a glass of wine."

"Bernie's driving," Mary said quickly, "but I wouldn't mind." She didn't look over to see her friend's expression, but she didn't need to.

"I heard that poor old Paul is out of hospital."

Mary nodded. "He seems to be on the mend, thank goodness."

"Take more than a heart attack to kill the old man," Nevyn said.

"Heart attack?"

"Yeah, that's what I heard it was."

Mary didn't challenge that. Not yet. "I guess you must have known each other quite well."

"Not really. Our paths crossed over the years."

"Funny, I heard that you had a wee fallout."

193

The man wasn't stupid. "Did you? Just what exactly are you investigating here?"

"Oh, you don't need to worry. In fact, it looks like Paul Gunn's little episode was brought on by an accidental overdose."

"Overdose? Of what?"

Was it her imagination, or did Nevyn look worried?

"I can't really say," Mary said, taking a sip of the wine. She never really drank the stuff, but this was all right. She was more of a fizz girl normally, whatever was on the three for two offer.

"But you wouldn't be investigating if there wasn't something going on?"

Bernie leaned forward. "Maybe we thought there might be a scandal there somewhere. I mean, you put half a dozen celebrities together and there's got to be some dirty secrets, right?"

"Well, I can only speak for myself, but we're not quite as exciting as the papers make out."

"Is that right?" Mary asked. She had another, larger sip of wine. "I guess we were hoping you could give us some pointers."

Nevyn moved his chair closer to hers. Mary had a funny feeling he was trying to flirt with her, and she had to admit she was a little flattered. Unlike the other 'celebrities' from the

Cook-Off, Nevyn wasn't just Invergryff famous. He was *telly* famous.

"I'm intrigued by the idea of a private detective," Nevyn said, offering her another dazzling smile. "How does one go about such a thing?"

"Get divorced and be desperately in need of a job," Mary said with a laugh. "But I like to think that I've got a bit of a knack for it."

"I'm sure you have," Nevyn said. "I bet people tell you every secret they have. But you see, I have nothing to tell."

"That's not strictly true, is it," Bernie said. She pulled her phone out of her pocket and showed him the video. "This happened right under your nose and you never said anything about it. That sounds like a whopper of a secret to me."

Nevyn's face went redder than the wine. "Where did you get this?"

"It's some of the unedited footage from the director. And it won't be too long until someone sends it to the police."

"It's not what it looks like," Nevyn said quickly.

"Then you didn't see One-shot Sam poisoning Paul Gunn's coffee?"

"Poison? God no. Look, the lad told me he was going to play a prank. Put a roofie in Gunn's drink. He thought it would be funny."

"And you thought that was okay?"

Nevyn ran a nervous hand through his hair. "I didn't think it would do any harm. I thought Gunn would stagger about a bit, make a tit out of himself, that sort of thing. Then when he collapsed, I just kept quiet. I didn't want to get the kid in trouble."

"Or yourself," Mary prompted.

"Why did you hate him so much?"

"Because he had an affair with my wife," Nevyn said. "Twenty years ago when I was new and looked up to guys like him. Six months he was shagging her for before I found out about it."

"Yep, that'd do it," Bernie said.

"What happens now? Will it all come out?" Nevyn's face was much less attractive when it was screwed up in self-pity.

Bernie shrugged. "You'll find out."

Five minutes later Mary and Bernie were back in the car.

"What a prat," Mary said. She was feeling a little light-headed as she'd made sure to down the wine before they left. "At least One-shot Sam is a young idiot. Nevyn should have known better."

"Yeah, looks like that Sam is in big trouble. We've just got to find out if he planned to hurt Gunn, or if it was meant to be just a joke."

"I wonder if any of the other celebs saw anything," Mary said,

196

thinking out loud. "I'd hate to cause trouble for this young lad if it really was just a prank."

"The only ones that I can't get hold of are the rugby player, but he's back in England already, and Loretta Shakespeare."

"Who was she again?"

"The ballet dancer. I don't suppose one of your kids would fancy doing a trial lesson?"

Mary twirled her hair around her fingers. "Let me think. Lauren's not well enough. Vikki is going through a tomboy phase, she's just got into monster trucks so I think ballet is out. Peter... well, probably not a good idea."

"Yeah. Even if the woman murdered someone she doesn't deserve to try and teach your Peter to dance."

The statement was so painfully true that Mary couldn't even be offended. "I'll try Johnny. If I bribe him with a chocolate bar for afterwards he'll probably do it."

"Great. I'll get on to Ewan and find out where this Sam hangs out."

"I still think we should tell the police," Mary reminded her.

"We will," Bernie said. "We'll just make sure we do it when it suits us. And Alice. Just finding out who put the roofie in Gunn's drink doesn't help with who stole the evidence bag."

"That's true."

"I'll get Liz to search for connections between One-shot Sam and our suspicious police officers. If there's anything there to find, she'll get it for us."

"While looking after a newborn," Mary said.

"I'm sure she'll manage. I was back at the gym when Ewan was four weeks old."

"Yes, but you're not normal, Bernie."

"Thanks."

"It wasn't a compliment."

Chapter 31: Alice

Alice was making a sandwich when the doorbell rang. Her mum was out at work so it was probably just a delivery. They knew to leave things at the back door, or flung into the porch, so she didn't bother going to get it. It was a cheese and pickle sandwich and she had been looking forward to it all morning.

The doorbell rang again.

"God dammit," Alice said, putting down the knife. She made her way to the front door and yanked it open.

"Hi."

"Hi, Brooklyn like the bridge. What are you doing here?"

He tried out a tentative smile. "I was going to check up on Paul Gunn, make sure he got home okay. I was wondering if you fancied coming."

"Sure," Alice said. "Just give me a minute."

"Is that a Firefly hoodie?"

Alice looked down at her chest. "Oh yeah. My friend gave it to me."

"I used to be a big fan of Inara when I was younger."

"Who? Sorry, I've never seen it."

Brooklyn blushed. Again. It was becoming a habit. "It doesn't matter."

"I'll go and get changed and I'll be down in five minutes, okay?"

Just over five minutes later, Alice climbed into Brooklyn's car.

"Did you bring a snack?"

"Cheese and pickle. Want half?"

"No thanks. Gluten intolerant."

Alice chewed her crust. "Like, proper coeliac or just makes you a bit bloated?"

Brooklyn kept quiet and turned the radio on. Gotcha, Alice thought.

"So is this an officially sanctioned visit?" Alice asked.

"I asked Detective Sergeant O'Connor if it would be okay, and she said fine as long as I didn't upset anyone. I told her about the evidence bag."

"Huh, I bet she told you to forget about it."

"No, actually, she said to make sure I noted it on the file. I think she's all right, that O'Connor."

Alice sniffed. He could be right, but she didn't see the Detective Sergeant going out of her way to help her out.

"Well, someone moved that evidence bag. If it wasn't you

then it was O'Connor, Laidlaw or Morrison."

"What do you mean, 'if it wasn't me'?"

Alice shrugged. "You could be being nice to me to put me off the scent."

"That's not why I'm being nice to you."

Oh dear. Alice wasn't very good at flirting, so in a panic she said: "I hope you're not getting fresh with me."

"Getting fresh? How old are you?"

"Um, I spend a lot of time hanging out with older ladies."

"From the war?"

Alice pointed. "That's the Gunn house. Why don't you pull over and stop harassing me."

"Now you're being fresh," Brooklyn grinned and turned off the engine.

The Gunns' house was a large seventies-style building on a leafy street that had to be one of the most expensive in the area. It had a real life gravel driveway and garden gnomes flanking the front door. Brooklyn rang the bell, but there was no answer.

"Did you tell them we were coming?"

Brooklyn shook his head. "No. I guess I assumed they would be in. Isn't Gunn supposed to be recuperating?"

"I thought so. Maybe he didn't get out of the hospital after all."

"Yeah. Sorry I dragged you all the way over here for nothing."

Mary looked up at the house. "You know, seeing as we're here, why don't we have a quick look around?"

"I don't think we should —"

"Just outside. Look, there's a gate to the back garden. Let's just have a wee shuftie."

She opened the gate and was relieved to see Brooklyn skulk in after her. There was hope for the boy yet. The back garden was very smart, with lots of brightly coloured flowers in hanging baskets and glazed pots. A large lawn had been recently mown and someone had swept the leaves into neat little piles. Given that Gunn had been in hospital, either his wife was a keen gardener or they paid someone for its upkeep. Judging by the size of the house they weren't short of cash.

"What are you doing?"

"I just want to have a quick peek in the windows," Alice said as she cupped her hands around her eyes and stared through the patio doors. The kitchen was neat and tidy, nothing to see there. She went over to the other window which looked into some sort of study. This was a little less tidy, but still empty.

Alice took a couple of steps backwards and looked at the upper floor. There were three windows up there, all with the curtains closed.

"Don't suppose you fancy shimmying up a drainpipe?"

Brooklyn didn't laugh. "I'm not sure if you're joking or not, but the answer is no."

"Pity."

"Let's head off. We can stop by later on and try and catch them at home."

She didn't like to admit defeat, but there didn't seem to be anything else they could do. With a sigh, she followed Brooklyn out of the gate and back around the front.

"I'm going to try the front door one last time," Alice said, giving it a thumping knock. There was still no movement from within the house. She squatted down and looked through the letterbox. Then she narrowed her eyes and looked again.

"Is that… is there a foot sticking out there? Look, at the bottom of the stairs."

She stepped to one side so that Brooklyn could join her.

"I think… it could be." He stood up.

Alice dropped down and looked through once more. "Oh no."

Brooklyn was already on the phone to the station. As he was telling them the address and asking for an ambulance, Alice looked for something to break the glass on the door.

"Here, let me," the Constable wrapped his coat around his arm and after turning his head away smashed his elbow through the glass. He knocked the broken shards aside and reached in to grab the key and open the door.

Alice rushed in to find the body. But not the one she expected.

"It's Mrs Gunn," Alice said, trying not to look at the awkward positioning of the woman's limbs. Her body was sort of crumpled on the bottom two stairs and there was dried blood around her temples.

"Check for a pulse," Brooklyn said, reminding her of the procedure. "I'm going to clear the rest of the house."

She knelt down beside the woman and pressed her fingers to the wrist that was already cold. Nothing. It looked like she had been dead for a few hours at least.

While Brooklyn checked out the upstairs, Alice cleared the kitchen and the living room, calling out 'Police' as she did so. There was no one there.

"Up here!" Brooklyn yelled and Alice sprinted up the stairs.

The Constable was in what looked like the master bedroom where the body of Paul Gunn was lying in the bed, eyes closed.

"Is he…"

"He's breathing, but I can't wake him up. I've checked the rest of the house and there's no one else here. What the hell is going on?"

Alice was just as confused. "I don't know. Has he been

poisoned again? And why would anyone kill his wife?"

"She looked like she could have fallen down the stairs," Brooklyn said. "Maybe it was an accident."

"One hell of a coincidence, don't you think?"

"Definitely. Man, the Superintendent is going to do his nut when he finds out you were here."

"I'm sorry," Alice said, just realising how much trouble was heading for Brooklyn. "I could leave now."

"No, that would make things worse. I'll explain everything. Don't worry."

The sound of sirens came from outside and Alice ran downstairs to let them in. The paramedics went up to see Mr Gunn once they had checked that his wife was beyond help. Alice was left alone once more with the woman.

She looked down at the late Mrs Gunn and realised she didn't even remember her first name. It made her jaw clench in anger. If only someone had taken the missing evidence seriously at the start, then this might never have happened.

But something else was edging aside the anger, and that was a sense of guilt. Alice hadn't told any of the police officers about the video footage of One-shot Sam. And she bloody well should have done. Because what if he was connected to this poor woman at the foot of the stairs? What if she could have stopped this happening?

The front door opened once more to let DS O'Connor in.

205

"Alice? What the hell are you doing here?"

Alice forced her shoulders straight. "That's a long story. But I've got something else to tell you first and you're not going to like it."

Chapter 32: Walker

All hell was breaking loose at Invergryff police station. The Paul Gunn case which had been considered closed had lurched back into life in the most dramatic fashion.

Alice was now on an official suspension. Walker hadn't managed to speak to her to get the full details, but the gossip in the station said that she had had evidence of the poisoner and not shared it until after Mrs Gunn was dead.

The most surprising news was that a warrant had been issued for the arrest of One-shot Sam. The kid didn't seem to have any reason to hurt Gunn, and apparently he was saying the whole thing was a prank gone wrong. But now that Emily Gunn was dead, that put rather a different spin on things.

The first thing that they needed to do was to interview Paul Gunn himself, now that he had woken up from a heavily sedated sleep. They had a family liaison officer at the house who had broken the news of his wife's death. It was a horrible job and Walker was selfishly glad that he hadn't had to do it. The next task on the list was to arrange for a senior officer to head the investigation into the suspicious death.

Luckily for Walker, that was Detective Inspector Macleod, currently on his way down from the islands. Walker had worked with Macleod on several occasions and they had a healthy mutual respect.

They had decided to do the interview at Gunn's house. No

one was sure if the man was fit enough to attend the police station in the first place. A community nurse had arrived to look after him until some permanent arrangement could be made. This meant that Walker had to do a quick run over to the airport to pick up the Inspector so that they could get started.

DI Macleod had looked even more knackered than usual when they picked him up. "Gale force winds up in Stornoway," he had said as Walker had driven him to the house. "I was puking all the way down to Glasgow."

"You won't be wanting one of these then," Walker said, pulling a pack of biscuits out of his bag. Macleod was notorious for being grumpy when he hadn't eaten.

"Just give me two," Macleod said, holding out his hand. "Seeing as they're not the chocolate-covered ones."

"You said last time not to buy them again," Walker reminded him. "You said you were starting your diet by skipping chocolate on biscuits."

"Well, I put on two kilos last month so I might as well have the fancier biscuits."

"I'll remember that for next time."

"Can you stop talking about biscuits," O'Connor complained from the back seat. "I'm trying to get through to the pathologist. We're hoping to get a slot for the post-mortem this evening. And talking about biscuits is a little distracting."

"Senior officer here," Macleod said, giving her a wink in the
208

mirror. "And I pull rank."

O'Connor gave him a singular gesture from the back.

"Rude," DI Macleod chuckled. "Look, there's the forensics guys. This must be the place."

They got out of the car and let the Constable manning the door know why they were there.

"He's upstairs with the nurse," Constable Flint said. "We've asked if he wants anyone with him, but he says no. They've already moved his wife and forensics have cleared the stairs so you can go on up."

It wasn't ideal, obviously, having to work a crime scene when one of the victims was upstairs, but sometimes policing was more complicated than it looked on the telly.

"What do you reckon," Macleod said, looking at the stairs. "An accident? Or something else?"

"I'll get the latest from the forensics lads," O'Connor said "See if they found anything interesting."

The DI nodded. "We'll go upstairs and speak to Paul Gunn."

The man looked just like he had in the hospital, pale and weak. A nurse was checking his blood pressure when they came in.

"We're sorry for your loss, Mr Gunn," DI Macleod said.

"I just can't believe it," the man said. "I can't believe she's gone."

"The officers that found you said you had been sedated."

Gunn nodded. "They gave me some strong sleeping pills to take. I had no idea that anything had happened until the paramedics woke me up."

"You had no idea that anything had happened to your wife?" Walker was finding it hard to believe that Gunn had simply slept through his wife falling down the stairs.

"No. I took the heavy-duty painkillers and I was out for the count. Do you think if I'd been awake, I could have saved her?"

Not likely, Walker thought, but he said, "I think she died very suddenly. If you had been awake it probably wouldn't have made any difference."

Gunn blew his nose. "That's some comfort at least."

"We'll need to move you out of here for a couple of days," Macleod explained. "Once you feel strong enough."

"I'd rather stay in the house," the man said, a flash of temper appearing.

"I know, but it will just be for a night or two so we can process this room."

"I'll book into a hotel. Nurse, when do you think I'll be able to leave?"

The nurse checked her paperwork. "You could go today, as long as you take your time and be sure to rest. There's nothing here that says you can't be moved. And being up on your feet is good for you."

"All right. If this young lady will help me arrange transport then I'll vacate the room for you today. But please, don't make a mess. My wife would have hated that."

"You didn't receive any threats since you left the hospital?" Macleod asked. "Your wife didn't mention anyone hanging around the house."

"No. I think... she wasn't too steady on her feet. A bit of arthritis, you see. I think she probably just fell."

Macleod leaned forward. "I'm afraid we can't make that assumption, Mr Gunn, especially considering your recent hospital stay."

"Another accident," Gunn said. "At least, that's what they told me earlier. Some kid put something in my drink. A young fool, but not worth charging him. I'd like to just forget all about it."

Macleod caught Walker's eye, knowing fine well that that wasn't how it worked. If the Procurator Fiscal decided there was a case for charging the lad then it didn't matter whether Gunn wanted to go ahead with it or not.

They left Gunn and his nurse making arrangements for his hotel transfer and went down the stairs to catch up with O'Connor.

"Pretty good service from the NHS," Walker said. "I didn't realise nurses made hotel reservations."

211

O'Connor shook her head. "No, that's a private nurse. Name's Debbie Macintosh, I was talking to her earlier."

"I guess he's got the money to go private," Walker said.

DI Macleod checked his phone. "Time to head back to the station. One-shot Sam is going to be picked up in the next hour for questioning. We'll have to wait and see if he's going to be charged with murder, attempted murder or assault. Either way, it should be an interesting interview."

Chapter 33: Bernie

Alice wasn't answering her phone. Bernie found this very selfish. She wanted to tell her niece what they had found out from the newsreader. Nevyn had confirmed exactly what they had seen on the video and they were now in a position to do something about it.

"Matt says Lauren is still sleeping," Mary said, checking her phone. "So I could probably do another hour or so. Are we still stopping off for doughnuts on the way home?"

"No," Bernie said as they neared the centre of Invergryff. "We were never getting doughnuts. I just said that to make sure you came with me."

"What?"

"Deal with it. Now I think we should go and chat to One-shot Sam."

"I thought you said we weren't going to. That we should wait until we had more evidence or we might spook him."

Bernie raised an eyebrow. "Did I say that?"

"Yes."

"Well, things have changed. I've been thinking about it and it's not like he's a flight risk. That sort of person can't spend five minutes without messaging the whole world about where they are and what they're doing. For example, Ewan just texted me to say that good old Sam is opening a new gaming café today right here in Invergryff."

"And we're going there now."

"That's right."

"Without stopping for doughnuts.

"Yep."

Mary sighed. "Anyone ever tell you you're a cruel woman, Bernadette Paterson?"

Bernie didn't feel the need to reply to a question with such an obvious answer. Instead they drove on in silence until they found a parking space in the centre of town.

"I didn't know there was a new café here," Mary said, getting that look in her eyes that appeared whenever anyone mentioned the words 'pistachio éclair'.

"It opened last month. Ewan dragged me into it. Somehow he persuaded me to spend twenty quid on a box of Pokemon cards. Don't see why they need a celebrity now when they've already opened the bloody place."

"I guess it's like the Queen."

"What?"

"You know, a birthday and an official birthday. So this is an official opening."

Bernie shrugged. "Just as long as they won't be expecting me to pay for any more rubbish."

They rounded the corner only to see a massive queue in front of the new café.

"Looks like One-shot Sam is a popular guy," Mary said, joining the end of the queue.

"What the hell do you think you're doing," Bernie said, grabbing her arm and marching them to the front of the line. "We're here on official business and I'll be damned if I'm going to wait in line."

With Mary grumbling next to her, Bernie pushed her way past the waiting customers and into the café.

"Hey, there's a line, you know," a man with a superhero t-shirt on called out.

"We're with One-shot Sam," Bernie said.

"Part of his entourage," Mary said, pulling the door shut after them.

"Entourage?"

"I think I heard it on X-factor."

"Nice."

Once inside the café they didn't have any more problems as everyone assumed they had already been through the queue.

One-shot Sam was sitting at a small table in the corner where he was signing baseball caps and charging thirty quid for the privilege.

"Hello, we're huge fans of yours," Bernie said, elbowing past a man in a Return of the Jedi t-shirt.

"Yeah, big fans," Mary said.

One-shot Sam looked from one to the other, his expression slightly bemused. "All right. You want a hat?"

"Wow, that hat is totally hyper. I bet you're spamming Twitch right now," Mary was grinning inanely at the lad.

"What are you doing?" Bernie asked

"It's gamer speak. I looked it up. Am I right, bruh?"

"You need to stop now," Bernie said.

"What a noob," Mary winked at One-shot Sam, who looked horrified.

"Yeah, your friend's right. You should stop now."

Mary made a huffing sound and crossed her arms.

"We wanted to talk to you about Paul Gunn," Bernie said quickly. "We're private investigators."

One-shot Sam wasn't very good at keeping his face neutral. Bernie had never seen anyone look so guilty. "What, that old guy? That was well scary how he just collapsed. Too much cholesterol no doubt."

"I don't think it was cholesterol that did it," Bernie said, holding out her phone to show One-shot Sam a still from the video that showed him with his hand hovering over the man's cup.

"I don't… It's not what it looks like."

"Really? What is it, then?"

One-shot Sam's bravado had disappeared. His right leg was jittering and his face was that of a scared little kid. "I thought it would be funny, okay? He was a prick, so I thought if I popped a pill in his drink then he would make a fool of himself. Only I didn't know that he'd already been drinking, did I? That newsreader Nevyn told me that afterwards. And he said I should keep my mouth shut or I would get in real trouble."

"You'd better confess," Mary told him. "Or it'll look worse when it all comes out."

"But he's all right, isn't he? I saw online that he got out of hospital, so no one needs to know."

Bernie was just about to tell him exactly why that sort of attitude wouldn't work, when there was a commotion at the door. She turned around to see several police officers walk into the café.

"Is this something to do with you?" Sam asked, jumping to his feet.

"No, we haven't told anyone…" Bernie moved to one side as a couple of burly Constables flanked the young man.

Bernie and Mary spotted Walker, who gestured to them to come outside.

"You better stay out of the way," he told them. "One-shot Sam is under arrest."

"What?" Bernie whispered to the man. "We've just been speaking with him. He said it was all just a prank."

Walker went quiet for a second, then he said. "Mrs Gunn is dead. That doesn't look like a prank to me."

Mary put her hands to her mouth in shock, but Bernie was already processing what the police officer had said. One-shot Sam came out of the café with a police officer on either side. The put him into the back of the van, amid boos from the people in the queue.

"I don't think that boy is a killer," Bernie said.

"Then you better keep sticking your nose in," Walker said quietly as the police van drove away. "Because if he is innocent, that lad is in big trouble."

Chapter 34: Mary

Mary was heading to ballet class with her younger son Johnny. Bernie was in crisis mode, off to meet Alice and find out exactly what was going on. Mary could have gone to help, but she'd had to pay for a month of lessons in advance and she was determined not to waste the money.

Being nearly eight, Johnny hadn't been too keen to attend. Mary had spent the entire car journey telling him that ballet was not 'just for girls' and that there were plenty of male ballet dancers making loads of money from it.

"Like who?" Johnny asked, his arms folded across his chest.

"The main guy in Billy Elliot," Mary had said. "And... well, there must be loads I just can't check on my phone while I'm driving."

"Don't want to be a ballet dancer," Johnny said for the tenth time.

"It's hardly Swan Lake," Mary said. "It'll just be a bit of dancing around with some other kids. It'll be good exercise."

"Don't want to be a swan," Johnny said. "Want to be a ninja."

"You can be both!" Mary said, pulling into a parking place. "That's the wonder of the modern world. Now be quiet and put your leggings on."

By the time they got into the class, Johnny had cheered up a little. He was not – as he and Mary had both feared – the only boy there, and he went over to play with the two other male children in the corner.

"You must be Mrs Plunkett," Loretta Shakespeare said, coming over with her hand held out. She was just as skinny as Mary remembered but much taller than she had seemed at the Cook-Off. With her slim figure and excellent cheekbones, Loretta could have been a supermodel. Mary felt like a Christmas pudding in comparison.

"Hi, thanks for taking us at short notice."

"Oh, we're always glad to have more boys in the class. You never know, your Johnny might be a natural."

They both looked over at the child in question who seemed to have got one foot stuck on the bar and was having to be helped to get down again.

"Or if not it's good exercise," Loretta added. "My assistant Wyn will be taking the class, so you and I could go upstairs and fill in the paperwork if that's all right."

"Great," Mary said, giving Johnny a wave.

She followed the other woman to a small office where she was given the usual book of paperwork for children's activities (full medical history, allergies, eye colour and shoe size for a start).

"Have you had this school for a long time?" Mary asked.

"Just over twelve years. I started it when I retired from dancing myself. We've had more than a dozen former pupils go on to the Conservatoire in Glasgow, you know."

"That's brilliant," Mary said, well aware that her son would probably not be heading in that direction.

"Can I give you these additional forms in case we do school trips?"

Mary made her way through the forms that seemed to mainly be a list of eye-watering expenses she would be expected to cover.

"I saw you at the Cook-Off the other day," Mary said.

Loretta sighed. "What a nightmare that was. I only did it as a favour to the Director as they needed the bodies. Oh, sorry, that was a poor choice of phrase."

"It's all right. At least Paul Gunn pulled through in the end."

Loretta shifted in her seat. "Yes, I was glad to hear that."

"It's good that he's at home recovering," Mary said, probing at what seemed to be a weak point.

"Yeah," Loretta was staring down at the table.

Mary leaned closer to her. "Is something wrong?"

"No. Not at all. It's just… Well, you're going to think I'm being silly."

"I'm sure I won't."

Loretta shivered. "I just don't think he's quite the nice guy that everyone was making out."

"He didn't try and chat you up, did he?"

"No, nothing like that. It was the weirdest thing. We were sort of milling about before the show was due to start and I noticed that he was dragging one foot a little when he walked. Dancers notice these sorts of things. Most people wouldn't even realise. There can be all sorts of reasons for a foot to drag; muscular, arthritis, or another medical condition. Anyway, I suggested that he might want to see a physio. I've got an amazing one, totally saved my back and I was going to recommend her. But he just lost it."

"What do you mean, lost it?"

"It came out of nowhere. All of sudden he was up in my face, shouting at me, saying I needed to mind my own business, that he would sue me, of all things. I just stood there. I guess I should have stood up for myself, but he was freaking me out. Anyway, after a minute or so he stormed off. I was still shaking when I had to go out on that stupid stage."

"No one else mentioned Gunn having a temper," Mary said.

"I wouldn't have believed it myself. Five minutes later he was fine. I avoided him for the rest of the day, and then he collapsed. I did wonder if he was starting to feel ill, but that's no excuse for going off on one like that."

"It must have been horrible," Mary said.

Loretta shrugged. "It just came out of the blue. You know, you expect the odd aggressive guy on a night out or walking on a dodgy street. But not like that, not when he seemed so nice just a minute before."

She checked her watch. "I better get back downstairs. Will we go and find out how Johnny got on?"

They could hear the screams before they entered the room. One quick look at the scene showed Mary that her son was never going to be in Swan Lake.

"I didn't even know that we had a hose in here," Loretta said, turning off the tap in the bathroom.

"I'm really sorry," Mary said on behalf of her son who didn't look sorry at all.

"I don't normally do refunds, but I'll send your money back for the month."

"Thanks," Mary said, ushering Johnny out the door.

"You're welcome," Loretta replied, bolting the door behind them.

Chapter 35: Alice

Alice knew that her time in the Specials was over as soon as they arrested One-shot Sam. She had screwed up. With the evidence bag, she had known it wasn't her fault. When it came to sitting on the evidence about One-shot Sam, it definitely was.

"You know that you should have told us about the video," MacKinnon said. He was being kind to her and that was making it worse.

"Yes sir. I made a mistake."

"You certainly did. I'm afraid that we will have to go down the formal disciplinary route this time."

She managed a smile. "There's no need for that. I've already emailed my resignation."

MacKinnon couldn't hide his relief. "Well, if you think it's for the best."

"I would like to work my shifts this week if that's okay. I wouldn't want to leave anyone short-staffed."

"I suppose that would be all right," MacKinnon said, with some reluctance. "As long as you stay in the office. That means that Sunday will be your last shift."

"Yes sir."

MacKinnon stood up to indicate she was being dismissed and held out his hand. "I'm sorry it ended this way. I wish you all the best for the future."

"Thanks."

When she left the police station she drove to the other end of town and parked up on a leafy suburban street.

Alice had called an emergency meeting of the WWC and to her delight Liz had offered to host. Liz's house was definitely the nicest. The woman had been in finance before she quit to be an investigator full time and her husband was an optician. Mary and Bernie's two houses could both have fitted inside Liz's detached place with double garage.

The other bonus was that since Liz was breastfeeding she wasn't stinting on the snacks.

"I've ordered pizzas," Liz said when Alice walked into the living room, placing several bowls of crisps on the table. "If Bernie says anything she can take it up with baby Isioma. She's feeding all night at the moment and I need the carbs."

Alice grabbed a handful of crisps. "I'm starving. I've spent half the day at the police station and some idiot got rid of all the vending machines."

The doorbell rang and Alice got up to let Bernie and Mary in.

"Where's my baby girl?" Bernie asked when they walked in.

"Sleeping upstairs," Liz said, pointing to the video monitor. "You won't have to wait long to see her. She's been waking up every hour."

"Probably dying to see her Auntie Bernie. What happened to the protein snacks I left you last time?"

"They tasted like ass, Bernie."

"Charming."

"If you're not going to eat those crisps then pass the bowl over," Mary said. "My mum is watching Lauren and Bernie's Finn's agreed to take the others. Poor Lauren was trying to do gymnastics in the living room when I left. She's definitely struggling with the whole 'rest and recuperate' thing."

The doorbell rang again.

"That'll be the pizza," Liz said, jumping up and collecting the boxes.

"Ooh, gimmee," Alice said as they all crowded in. With one exception.

"I suppose I could have one slice," Bernie said. "Got any with anchovies?"

Liz passed her the single piece of pizza and they all watched in fascination as the woman chewed a tiny piece.

"I am the master of my own body," Bernie said when she caught the others staring at them. "And I've brought a fruit salad for after."

Reassured that Bernie hadn't been possessed by a carb-eating demon, Alice explained why she had brought them all together.

"I can't believe you resigned," Mary said.

Alice shrugged. She had had a few hours to come to terms with it and was feeling remarkably okay. "They might not have sacked me, but I would always have been the woman that messed up the case. And if it turns out that Mrs Gunn was attacked by One-shot Sam then I might be responsible for worse than that."

"I still don't think that kid could kill anyone," Mary said.

Bernie wiped her hands on a napkin. "What's the latest from the police station?"

Mary shrugged. "Walker only managed a quick call. They're going to interview One-shot Sam soon, but I just can't see how he was involved in Mrs Gunn's death."

"Do we know if she was attacked or not?"

"No. Even the police don't know. Walker said he was waiting for the pathologist's results, but he didn't sound too hopeful. I guess it's hard to tell if someone fell down the stairs or if they were pushed."

Alice sighed. "I can't get anyone from the station to talk to me. Even Brooklyn is avoiding my calls. I can't help but feel like if we could work out who took the missing evidence it might be key to this whole story."

"Ah, I might be able to help with that one. Just let me find my laptop." Liz lifted a pile of baby clothes, then a pile of nappies and wipes. "Here it is."

They waited while she typed something into the computer.

"So I wasn't getting anywhere with the connections. There was nothing financial to connect anyone from the celebrity list with the list of police officers. And then I saw something weird. One of the celebs had an account with a cryptocurrency exchange. And one of the police officers had opened an account with the same exchange on Sunday."

"I guess One-shot Sam might be into crypto," Alice said. "He's the right age group."

"It wasn't One-shot Sam."

They looked at the name.

"But that doesn't make sense."

"I know." Liz shrugged. "I just find the links. It's your job to explain them."

Chapter 36: Walker

They didn't manage to interview One-shot Sam until Friday morning. At first the young man had been kicking off, saying he wasn't going to say anything without a solicitor. Then when they got him a solicitor, he still refused to do the interview, saying that he wasn't 'emotionally stable' enough. Even the solicitor was getting frustrated with the kid and Walker heard him say 'arrogant prick' under his breath when Sam complained about the quality of the police station coffee. A night in the cells seemed to calm him down, however, and first thing in the morning he asked to speak to the Inspector.

Walker tagged along, only to see that it didn't go quite how Macleod had hoped.

"I want to speak to the scary woman and her funny friend."

"Who?"

Walker cleared his throat. "Um, I think he might be thinking about Bernadette Paterson and my girlfriend, sir."

"Those two? No way."

Sam folded his arms. "I won't tell you pigs nothing. But I'll speak to them."

And that was that. No amount of cajoling from the police officers or his solicitor could get One-shot Sam to say another word. Which meant by nine o'clock Mary and Bernie were happily ensconced in the family room at the station, eating some chocolate biscuits that had appeared from nowhere. Or at least one of them was. The other appeared to be gnawing on a dog chew.

"What is that?" Walker asked.

"Beef jerky. High protein. You should try some."

"No thanks," Walker said, hoping that Bernie wouldn't smell the fast food breakfast he had grabbed on the way over. He had eaten it in the car and he was sure there was some grease on his jumper.

"We've got the interview room ready," Macleod said, coming into the room. "Now I want to make it clear that I am leading the interview. You are here as an adjunct to the official process. It is highly irregular, and I don't want you doing anything that could endanger the investigation."

"I thought the lad said he would only speak to us," Bernie said.

Walker looked up at the ceiling, anywhere but meet the DI's eyes.

"Well, yes, but I will be facilitating your involvement," Macleod said, his face growing red.

"I'm sure you will be an excellent facilitator," Bernie said, her voice dripping with sarcasm. "Now let's not keep the kid waiting. I've got a kettlebell class at eleven."

One-shot Sam didn't look like he had slept much. For all his tough talk, he looked like a little kid when they walked into the

230

interview room. He was slumped down in his chair and his eyes were bloodshot.

Macleod introduced them all for the tape, managing to grimace his way through the introduction of 'Mary Plunkett and Bernadette Paterson from the Wronged Women's Co-operative, assisting in the interview.' He did stutter a little over One-shot Sam's real name, which turned out to be Samuel Dixon Wallace, a name that didn't quite suit his trendy appearance.

While they waited, Bernie was practically preening herself and Walker just had to hope that they would get through the interview before Macleod spontaneously combusted.

"You wanted to speak with these ladies present," Macleod said once the legal requirements were out of the way. "Why don't you tell us what happened?"

One-shot Sam put his head in his hands.

"I know it's scary," Mary said gently. "But you'll be in more trouble if you don't tell the truth. Why don't you start with the Cook-Off?"

"I only did it because he told me to," One-shot Sam said, in a voice that was close to a wail.

"Ah," Bernie nodded her head. "That makes sense. He told you to put the stuff in Gunn's drink?"

"Yes."

Walker looked from one to the other in confusion.

231

"Hang on a minute," Macleod said. "Someone told you to drug Gunn? Well, you better tell us who."

"It was Nevyn Petty," Mary said quietly.

"Who… the newsreader? What's he got to do with this?" Walker asked.

"And just how did you two already know that," Macleod asked, his voice dangerously calm.

"We only found out last night," Mary explained. "Or at least, we found a clue that Nevyn might be involved. We hadn't had a chance to tell you yet."

"What the… All right. Let's focus on our current suspect for now, shall we? Can you tell us exactly what happened on the Sunday?"

Sam picked at the nails on his right hand. "I didn't want to do the Cook-Off at first. But my publicist said it would, like, get me to a new audience? I dunno, it felt like it was just a load of old people. And I was saying to that newsreader guy before we went in that I wanted to shake things up a bit, you know? And then he says, why don't we make things a bit more fun? Why don't we put something in that old loser's drink?"

"He gave you the pills?"

"No, that was the funny thing. He said it won't even be that bad because they were Paul Gunn's own pills anyway. And quick as you like, he reaches into the man's bag – it was sitting in the locker room with all our stuff – and pulls out some pills. He said they were sleeping pills or something, that he would just nod off during the show. And it would be a bit of a laugh."

Walker was making notes. "You're sure these were Paul Gunn's own pills?"

"Yeah, they came out of his bag. So I didn't think there would be any harm. But then it all went to crap, didn't it?"

"You never once thought of telling anyone when Gunn collapsed," Bernie said, her voice stern. "It might have helped his treatment."

Sam hung his head. "I was scared. Nevyn said it wouldn't make a difference, that the pills couldn't have caused a heart attack. I guess… I kind of wanted to believe him, so I did."

"All right, let's come to last night," Macleod said. "If it was all just a prank, why did you go back and attack Mrs Gunn."

"I didn't!" One-shot Sam jumped up out of his chair and his solicitor had to get him to sit back down. "Look, man, I told you about what happened with the guy's coffee. It was all a stupid mistake. I wanted to forget all about it, not go after him again. And why would I hurt his wife?"

"Maybe you went there to attack Paul Gunn and the wife tried to stop you. Or she startled you and you pushed her. You probably didn't intend to kill her."

"You're fitting me up," Sam shook his head. "I'm not going down for this. No way."

His solicitor leaned forward. "You don't seem to have any

physical evidence to suggest that my client was ever in the Gunn family home."

"Not yet," Macleod replied. "Our investigations are ongoing."

"Then I think my client has said enough for now."

One-shot Sam folded his arms. The rest of them left the room and walked into the corridor.

"It's clear as day that kid never killed anyone," Bernie said as soon as the door closed.

Macleod stiffened. "Funnily enough, we tend to not take advice from members of the public about whether or not to charge people. We can hold him for another couple of hours and we should have some more pathology results back on Mrs Gunn."

"You've had the autopsy by now, I suppose. Could we have a look at the report?"

The Inspector exhaled through his nose. "What do you think?"

"How about we tell you how we knew about the newsreader, and you give us a wee look at the post-mortem?"

For a minute, Walker thought that Macleod was going to throttle the woman, but then he sagged in submission.

"Fine. Tell me."

"Nevyn Petty has an account with a cryptocurrency exchange called 1XPchange. A friend of ours was looking for links to the cops that were in the room when the evidence bag disappeared. One of those officers opened an account with the same exchange the day of the Cook-Off."

"Could be a coincidence?"

Bernie shook her head. "According to my finance expert, there are thousands of these exchanges. The one that Nevyn used is quite specialised and not that many casual customers use it. Plus there's the timing."

"Okay, you've convinced me. Walker, you go and see this dodgy officer and see what they've got to same for themselves. Tread lightly. I'm going to take another look at the forensics on the Gunn house. I don't want to pull Nevyn Petty in until we've got a decent case against him. He seems the type that would run to the papers if there's a hint we've got anything wrong."

"Sure," Walker said.

"Can we come?"

"No," Macleod and Walker said in unison.

Chapter 37: Bernie

"Bernie?"

"Yes?"

"The Detective Inspector explicitly said that we weren't to have anything to do with Nevyn Petty."

"That's right."

Mary sighed. "So I suppose what I'm wondering is why we are sitting in the carpark of his hotel."

"I don't like being told what to do," Bernie said. She wished her friend would be quiet. She was trying to read the post-mortem report.

"I know, but it is a murder investigation."

"Is it? They haven't even decided on that one yet. I mean, take this post-mortem. It barely tells you anything."

Mary looked over her shoulder. Bernie kept scrolling through the document.

"I have no idea what any of these words mean," Mary said. "What's a contusion?"

"A bruise."

"Why don't they say so then?"

Bernie rolled her eyes. "Didn't you ever watch *Casualty*? Or *ER*?"

"No. And they didn't do many autopsies on *Doctor Who*."

"Well, it doesn't say anything definite. For the cause of death it lists 'traumatic brain injury' and 'multiple fractures' but there's nowhere on here that says if it was a murder or if the poor woman just took a tumble down the stairs. I get the feeling that if it wasn't for the fact that someone had already poisoned Paul Gunn then they wouldn't even be investigating."

Mary put her feet up on the glove compartment. "I can't believe One-shot Sam was stupid enough to put something into that drink. Just because Nevyn said it would make a good prank."

"He probably looked up to the newsreader. No matter how much they go on about 'streaming', these social media stars are always dying to get on the real telly. Maybe Nevyn promised him a slot on the news."

"That could well be it," Mary agreed. "I can't help feeling sorry for him. I mean, the police will probably see him as an arrogant criminal, but he's just a terrified kid."

"The problem is that terrified kids do really stupid things," Bernie said. "You know that as well as I do. Paul Gunn could have died that day because of One-shot Sam's stupidity."

Mary didn't say anything, but Bernie knew she could see the sense of it all. Just because the lad had shown remorse didn't mean that he wasn't guilty. And Bernie firmly believed that the guilty should be punished.

"What have you been learning about our Mr Petty," Bernie asked. She had tasked Mary with going back over the newsreader's online presence. There was something more going on here than a prank, and she was sure of it.

"Well, not much more than what the man told us himself. He said that Paul Gunn had an affair with his wife, but there's no evidence of it online. Nevyn's wife was called Susan Petty, born Susan Lourdes, and she died from cancer a couple of years ago."

"Any family."

"Yeah. It's kind of sad, really. They had one daughter but she died not long after the wife. She had some sort of long-term illness and she was only twenty. Her name was Lila."

"That is sad," Bernie said.

"It is. But none of that connects back to Paul Gunn. And if he was pissed off at Gunn for shagging his wife, then wouldn't he have done something about it at the time? Why wait twenty years to get your own back?"

"These things can fester," Bernie said. "I remember at the care home we had one man smack another over the head with a gravy boat because of what one had called the other's mother at the Queen's coronation."

Mary shook her head. "We're missing something."

238

A hand tapped on the window and Bernie jumped. She turned to see the ruddy face of Detective Inspector Macleod.

Reluctantly, she wound down the window.

"I'd ask you what you were doing here, Ms Paterson, but why do I get the feeling that I already know?"

"No law against parking here, is there?" Bernie asked.

Macleod gave her his best glare, but Bernie had been glaring at people her whole life, so she wasn't fazed.

"You just make sure you stay here, all right?" Macleod said finally.

"Sure thing, boss," Bernie grinned and watched the man and his fellow officers walk into the hotel.

"Maybe we should check out Nevyn's car," Mary said after a moment of silence. "I think it's the Beemer over there by the entrance."

"You're only trying to cheer me up because we can't get into the hotel," Bernie said.

Mary pinched her arm. "That's true. But I was thinking we could check the tyre treads, maybe match them with some at the Gunn house."

"Okay Nancy Drew," Bernie couldn't help but laugh.

"Maybe not then," Mary said, settling back into her seat. "I wouldn't mind a look in that car though. There might be a bloody knife in the glove compartment."

"No one was stabbed."

"Oh yeah. I forgot. What's that bumper sticker on the back windscreen?"

Bernie peered at the car. "I think it says support Huntington's Action. Some charity sticker."

"Huntington's," Mary repeated. "I've heard that somewhere recently. What is it?"

"A degenerative disease. Pretty poor prognosis. It's inherited, and there's no curative treatment. We had a few early admissions at the home. From when you're diagnosed you might be terminal within a decade, although some people live longer."

Mary had that look on her face, like her brain was whirring away.

"What is it?" Bernie asked.

"What would the symptoms be?"

"Well, it's a disease of the nerve cells. So gradually you lose skills like talking, walking… It's a degenerative brain disease. There's no cure."

"What about the early symptoms?"

Bernie wracked her brain. "It could show itself in all sorts of ways. You wouldn't know you had it until you did the proper test."

"What sorts of ways? Exactly."

240

"Well, it's often mistaken for dementia or Parkinsons. People might notice that they're slurring their speech, or that they're more clumsy than usual. The only way to know for sure is to do the genetic test."

"They might drag one leg a little," Mary said. "Or seem drunk when they were sober."

"Yes, just like that."

Mary smacked her hands on her thighs. "I think I've got it! Or... at least the shape of it. Let me check and see what killed Nevyn's daughter."

Bernie waited while Mary typed something into her phone.

"Got it! Her obituary says she had a 'long battle with Huntington's'."

It was annoying that Mary had worked something out that she hadn't. "Yes, well, we know that he supports the charity, so that's hardly a surprise."

"But what if Nevyn isn't her father at all?"

It was Bernie's turn to look shocked. "You're talking about Gunn? You think he was the father of the girl that died?"

Mary nodded. "Huntington's is hereditary, right? I think that Paul Gunn has Huntington's disease. The ballet dancer, Loretta, she noticed that he was dragging one side. When she told him he went completely off on one. And there was that video of him at the Christmas party where he was staggering about. I just assumed he was drunk, but it could be the early

241

symptoms, couldn't it?"

Bernie tapped her finger on the wheel. "I like it. It sounds like a plausible theory. But wouldn't the hospital have said something to the police about it? I mean, it would be a significant factor in his collapse."

"What if they didn't know?"

"It would be on his medical records."

"Maybe he didn't disclose it. I mean, didn't Walker say that Paul Gunn had a private nurse?"

Bernie shook her head. "I'm not sure that makes sense."

"Okay, maybe I need to work on that part. But listen, I've just looked up the treatment for Huntington's. Benzodiazepine is frequently prescribed to manage the symptoms."

"I think you might just have it," Bernie said. "But how the hell are we going to prove something like that?"

"I don't know."

"Neither do I. But I know one thing." She looked over to the hotel and saw Nevyn being escorted out by the police officers. "I think we've just found a hell of a good reason to get into that interview room."

Chapter 38: Mary

Before they went back to the station to speak to Nevyn Petty, Mary had nipped back home to check on Lauren. Once again she found Matt and Lauren sleeping together in her room. Well, at least her ex was getting a rest. Mary could have done with one herself. Between the hospital stay and the Paul Gunn case hotting up, she felt like she hadn't been able to breathe, let alone take a little nap, for ages.

She was just grabbing a cereal bar out of the cupboard when the doorbell rang.

Alarms bells were ringing as soon as she opened the door. A huge hulking figure stood in the doorway.

"Hello?"

"Gonna let me in, it's freezing out here."

"I don't know you," Mary said, her voice shrill. It had only been a few months ago when a criminal had forced his way into her home and threatened her children. And now here was this creepy guy. "What do you want?"

"I've got a bone to pick with you," the man said and he took a step towards her.

The blood was rushing in Mary's ears and she reached for the shelf next to the door, grabbing her special spray.

"Take that, arsehole!"

243

"Gnnnahhh," the man fell to his knees, clutching his eyes.

"Mary, no!"

Mary turned to see Walker running up the path.

"I got him," Mary shouted. "I got the creep!"

"That's not a creep. That's my brother."

It was Mary's turn to make a noise like a harpooned dolphin. "Oh god, I didn't know. He seemed… I thought he was threatening me."

"I should have told you he was coming," Walker said once they were inside. They were back in Mary's living room while his brother was upstairs in the bathroom flushing the pepper spray out of his eyes. The man hadn't even replied when she'd made him a shaky offer of a cup of tea.

"He said he had a bone to pick with me, so I thought it was a bad guy. You know, like before."

"Yeah. We had a fallout the other night. He doesn't approve of me going out with a woman with kids. Feels like he needs to protect me from you, can you imagine."

Mary squeezed his knee. "I am pretty scary, right?"

"Right. I mean, you were when you were wielding that bottle. You know that pepper spray is illegal, don't you?"

"It's not proper pepper spray," Mary showed him the bottle which had a distinctly homemade air about it. "It's a blend I made myself. Mainly cayenne, a bit of chilli pepper and a little bit of smoked paprika when I ran out."

"I guess that's good for Ru. I won't have to take him to A and E."

There was a groan from upstairs.

"Not that he'll appreciate it at the moment."

Mary pressed her knees together. She was more than a little embarrassed. "I made it after that time that horrible man broke into my house and threatened me. I felt so helpless, and I never wanted to feel that way again. I suppose I just overreacted."

Walker nodded. "Maybe you should look into some self-defence classes. Hopefully you'll never have to use them but it might make you feel a bit better."

"Sounds a bit too much like exercise."

"I've done them. There's no requirement to wear leggings."

She looked a little happier. "All right. I'll consider it. Might even be able to get Bernie to pay for it from expenses."

Her phone started ringing. "Speak of the devil, that'll be Bernie. Bloody hell, I'm meant to be interviewing Nevyn Petty in five minutes."

At that moment Matt came down the stairs, looking dishevelled. "What's going on?"

"Sorry Matt, I've got to go. Um, can you sort all this out?"

"Sure," Walker and Matt said at the same time, then glowered at each other.

Just perfect, Mary thought as she ran outside to her car. She drove as quickly as she could without endangering life and limb and was only slightly late when she got to the police station.

"Where've you been?" Bernie did not look happy. "Macleod is having kittens."

"Some minor drama at home," Mary said, trying to get her breath back.

"What's that smell?" Bernie asked.

The detectives had arrived and showed them along the corridor to the interview room.

"Probably pepper spray," Mary whispered. "I'll tell you later."

"Make sure you do," her friend replied. "Are you ready for the interview?"

"Sure. Why not. Confronting a murder will be easy compared to the day I've had."

Back in the interview room for the second time that day and Mary noted that it wasn't smelling any fresher. She took a sip of her tea and grimaced even though she had put an extra sugar in it. UHT milk was the pits.

It only took them a few minutes to fetch Nevyn Petty from the cells. The man was no longer looking as slick as he did on the telly. His stubble was showing and his hair was sticking up at the sides where he had been running his hands through it.

Mary was thinking she would probably make a dreadful police officer. She was a decent private investigator, she knew that, and she'd always had a way with people. But it was just that tendency for empathy that was currently causing her trouble. She didn't want to ask this poor man about his dead daughter, but that was exactly what Detective Inspector Macleod was doing.

"Your daughter passed away from Huntington's disease, is that right?"

"Yes. Two years ago."

"I suppose you're wondering why I've brought that up."

Nevyn shrugged. He had refused a solicitor, despite repeated offers. He looked like a beaten man.

"You have claimed to the lady on my left that Paul Gunn had an affair with your wife."

Mary offered Nevyn an apologetic smile.

"It's not a secret."

"It is possible, therefore, that Paul Gunn was the biological father of your child."

"More than possible," Nevyn sighed. "Although I only found out quite recently."

"Why don't you tell us about it?"

Mary watched the man rub his knuckles. "Where to start? I guess it started with the mood swings. Lila was about fifteen when we noticed them. Of course, we thought they were normal. Teenagers, right? And I was away so much with work that I didn't always see it."

He paused, reached for a glass of water and then continued, all without looking up. "The mood swings got worse. Much worse. She started struggling at school. We were looking into a possible autism diagnosis, but nothing quite seemed to fit. Then the falls began and we knew it was something else. But we were still hopeful, you know? That it might be something treatable. Something that she might get better from. But it wasn't."

Mary felt the pain that had struck her heart when she heard the word 'meningitis' in relation to her child. How much worse must it be to hear that your baby would suffer so much, and with no cure?

"To get a firm diagnosis of Huntington's they do a genetic test. It came back positive for Lila. But it showed something else. I had no genetic relation to my daughter."

He laughed. "It was the strangest thing. I wasn't even that angry. It seemed so... immaterial in comparison to what was going on with Lila. I asked my wife and she said she had always hoped it was me that was the father, but that there was a chance it was someone else."

"Paul Gunn."

He nodded. "A six-month fling, that resulted in a pregnancy.

So I got in touch with him, but he didn't want to know. No interest in a teenage daughter, especially one who was sick. I asked him about the Huntington's and he said he didn't have it. There was no history of it in his family. And that was it. Lila was getting much worse by that point, so I dropped it. I just didn't have the headspace, you know?"

Macleod kept his face impassive. "What changed?"

"I put on the car radio last month and tuned in to his station. I know, it was the weirdest thing. I didn't even realise who I was listening to at first. I don't know why I didn't just turn it off. Maybe I was just torturing myself, I don't know. Anyway, he was doing the late shift because one of his colleagues was sick or something and I noticed that as the show went on he started slurring his words a little. It could just be tiredness, but it was like a spark was lit. I had to know."

"You confronted him?"

"Two weeks ago. Yet again, he denied it. Said he did not have Huntington's. I just... the way he was lying to my face, I almost couldn't stand it. And then that Director, Josh, he called me up and told me about the Cook-Off."

"Did you plan to attack him?"

Nevyn's mouth turned down at the corners. "No. I don't know what I planned. But then he left the room at one point and I found some pills in his bag. I knew what they were for, of course. And the young lad saw me with them, and I panicked. I told him it would be fun to play a prank. I just wanted Gunn to show that he wasn't okay. That he was lying about the Huntington's. The disease that he had given my daughter."

Mary couldn't stay quiet any longer. "He wouldn't have known. I mean, when he slept with your wife, he didn't know he had Huntingtons."

"That's right," Bernie piped up. "Your daughter had juvenile Huntington's. Her illness progressed much more quickly. Gunn can only have been displaying symptoms recently."

"So? It doesn't help me any, does it?" Nevyn said. "He still killed her."

Mary shook her head. "I feel sorry for you. Of course I do. But you didn't have to kill an innocent woman just to cover it all up."

Nevyn's eyebrows shot up his forehead. "Kill her? You mean his wife? I didn't go near her. Look, I got the lad to put the drugs in his drink and I'll admit to that. I don't even care if they stick me in prison for it. But I would never kill someone. Not never."

"You realise that's a double negative," Bernie said, "and that means –"

"Not the time, Bernie," Mary jumped in. "Are you telling us the truth? You didn't kill Mrs Gunn?"

"No."

Macleod cleared his throat. "Thank you, ladies, for your interruptions, but I'm afraid Mr Petty, that we'll need more

250

than a 'no' to satisfy the procurator fiscal. Can you tell me where you were on Wednesday night?"

"In my hotel. All night." Was Mary imagining it, or did he look shifty? If he wasn't the killer then what the hell was he playing at?

"We'll check that out," Macleod said. "For the moment you'll be detained in our cells. I suggest you rethink your decision not to speak to a solicitor."

Chapter 39: Alice

Alice hadn't expected to be back at Laidlaw's house. Certainly not under these circumstances.

"Are you sure you want me to come?" she asked Walker and O'Connor.

"Walker thinks that you being here might unsettle Dan and make him more likely to talk," O'Connor said. "Besides, if he was the one that nicked that evidence bag then you deserve to know why."

"I'd like to know that too," Walker said. "Laidlaw's been a Special for longer than I've been a copper. What makes someone like that go bent?"

O'Connor held up several printed sheets. "His bank accounts give us some clues. Let's ring the bell and see what he has to say for himself."

When Laidlaw opened the door, Alice had thought he might break down there and then. Instead he crossed his large arms.

"I didn't realise I was hosting another games night."

"We're here officially, Dan. Can we come in?"

"Nothing stopping you." Laidlaw saved his best glare for Alice. "You been grassing me up to the full-timers, have you?"

This wasn't going at all how they had planned it. Walker gave her an apologetic glance.

"Maybe Ms Paterson could wait in the car."

Alice turned on her heel and heard the door shut behind her. She would have been deeply offended, if they hadn't already planned for this situation. Walker had put his radio on broadcast so that she would be able to hear exactly what was happening through the other set in the car. She settled down in the seat and held it up to her ear.

In the house, O'Connor was asking for a cup of tea, but Laidlaw wasn't having any of it.

"You didn't come here unannounced to have a cup of tea," he said.

"We're here about the missing evidence bag."

"You haven't found it yet, then?" Laidlaw asked.

"No," O'Connor said. "Because you took it."

Alice wished she could have seen the man's face. As it was, she just had to imagine it in the silence that followed.

"You reckon I did that?" Laidlaw said. He still wasn't giving up.

"You fancied a little dabble in crypto recently, didn't you?" O'Connor said. "Judging from your bank accounts, you've been investing heavily in the last few months. Lost a whole lot when Bitcoin dropped, but then you got a little windfall last weekend, didn't you?"

Laidlaw laughed. "Do you know, I actually believed them when they told me that account was untraceable? Didn't think the police accountants had it in them."

"We had some outside help," Walker said. "How did you get in contact with Nevyn Petty?"

"You make it sound like it was planned. It all just sort of happened. I found the Petty bloke near enough having a mental breakdown behind the stage. He was crying, real tears, you know? Kind of embarrassing. Then he says, he only wanted to show the guy up and he didn't mean to make him collapse. And then he looks at me and he asked if I could make it all go away. And then before I know it he's naming an amount that's more than I make in a year. In both my jobs. And enough to clear the goddamn credit card, for a start. So I just started listening."

"How did you get the bag out of there?" O'Connor asked.

Again, Laidlaw chuckled. The noise was really starting to irritate Alice.

"You make it sound like it was hard. I just took off my coat and swiped it. Then I took it out to the car wrapped in the coat and put it in the boot. Took less than a minute. It's still there. Of course, if you'd ordered a search when it went missing, you would have found it. But I knew you wouldn't bother."

Now it was O'Connor's face that Alice was wishing she could see. She guessed that the Sergeant would not be one bit impressed.

254

"Maybe there's a chance you could still come good," O'Connor said, even though Alice knew that she was bluffing. There was no way back for Laidlaw now. "I mean, I'm guessing you never knew it would end in murder."

"Of course I didn't. Bloody hell, is there a connection then?"

"Looks like there might be," Walker said.

"Well, I can't help you with that one. I didn't know about the murder until it was on the news."

"You realise if there's a connection you could do time for this."

"There's no connection."

"You better bloody hope not," Walker said. "And what about Alice? You were happy for her to take the fall for the missing evidence even though you knew all about it."

"She's just a kid. She's not exactly Specials material, is she? Come on, look at her. She's just wanting to make a few bucks before she goes off and starts her real life. But this is my real life. And I can't afford to lose it now."

Walker couldn't take it anymore. "You lost it the minute that you picked up that evidence bag. And that kid that you're talking about? She's shown exactly why she would make a great copper in the last week, by never letting people like you take advantage, not for one minute."

Laidlaw stiffened. "So it's like that, is it? You're just stringing me along?"

"I wanted to see how far you would take it," O'Connor said. "And we needed to get it all on record."

Now it was Laidlaw's turn to look horrified. "You're taping this?"

"Of course we're taping it," O'Connor snapped back. "And I'm going to hand the recording over to MacKinnon in the next hour or so. How about you go and speak to him yourself first? Might make things a bit easier."

"Screw you," Laidlaw said.

"I'm not an idiot," O'Connor said. "You can act as tough as you like, but I know why you wanted Alice to stay outside. You're embarrassed. Ashamed, even."

"You better get out before I throw you out," Laidlaw said and a few seconds later Alice watched the two police officers walk back to the car.

They climbed into the front seats, both of them looking like they'd been through the wringer.

"Wow, that was awful," O'Connor said.

"Do you think he'll talk to MacKinnon?" Walker asked.

"Aye. He's still holding onto the hope that they won't chuck him out. Fat chance of that happening."

"I was listening to the whole thing," Alice said. "Thanks for sticking up for me, Walker."

"I meant every word," the man replied. "You're a great Special,

256

and you'd make a brilliant copper."

Alice laughed. "No one told you I resigned today, did they?"

"What?"

"Yeah. I've been thinking about it for a while, and I knew that I would have to go through an official sanction for the One-shot Sam video. They might not have sacked me, but it felt like the right time to go."

"Oh." Walker didn't seem sure what to say. "I'm sorry to hear that."

"I'm not. It's time to move on and do something different."

"You're going to join your aunt's agency full time?" O'Connor asked.

"Maybe."

"Let's get back to the station," Walker said. "I want to know what's happening with Nevyn Petty. If we're lucky they've already got the case all sewn up."

Chapter 40: Walker

"We're going to release Petty," DI Macleod told Walker when they got back to the station.

"What? Why?"

"He's got an alibi for the time of Mrs Gunn's death."

"He said he was alone in his hotel room."

"Aye, he wasn't wanting us to know what he was up to. But when we showed him CCTV of his car leaving the car park, he had to come clean. It turns out that Nevyn did have an alibi. He visited a certain warehouse district to obtain some class C pick-me-ups. Once he realised he was about to be arrested for murder, he told us the name of his dealer. The man claimed not to have seen the newsreader, but luckily for Nevyn it had rained that night and we verified it was him by his tyre tracks."

"Tyre tracks?"

"Yeah, who knew?" Macleod said. "Anyway, your friends at the Wronged Women's Co-operative have come up with a new theory."

The Detective Inspector explained all about the Huntington's connection and the death of Nevyn's child.

"So Paul Gunn fathered the child and passed on an illness that he didn't even know he had."

"Yes."

Walker frowned. He felt like he was still trying to catch up. "If we're letting Petty go, then does that mean that we think Mrs Gunn's death was accidental?"

"That was my working theory. Until I had a chat with Bernadette Paterson."

"Oh really?" It wasn't often that the Inspector looked happy after an encounter with Bernie.

"It turns out that she has several friends that work as private nurses. And one of them worked with Paul Gunn's current nurse, Debbie Macintosh, and she has been boasting about how much money Gunn has been paying her. A lot more than a nurse would usually earn. So we've pulled her in."

"What about Gunn himself?"

Macleod shook his head. "The post-mortem on his wife was inconclusive. I want to tread very carefully. If it's going to be circumstantial evidence in this case then we need to make sure we've chased up every loose end before we get him in the interview room."

"Fair enough. When are you speaking to the nurse?"

"Right now. Want to join me?"

Technically Walker should have clocked off hours ago, but when a case was in the crucial stages like this one, Walker wouldn't want to be anywhere else.

"Of course."

As the nurse was not a suspect in anything, she was allowed to be questioned in one of the least cramped and not-even-very-smelly rooms off the main office.

"Miss Macintosh?"

"Yes?"

"Thank you for coming in."

"I can't stay long," the woman seemed very nervous, her hands twisting a paper tissue while she spoke. "Mr Gunn needs extra care at the moment."

"How long have you been working for him?"

"I… um, I wouldn't like to say."

DI Macleod raised an eyebrow. "You don't want to say when you started working for your employer? You know that we can check that."

Macintosh dabbed at her neck with the tissue. "I cannot discuss any aspect of my client's health with you. It's confidential."

"You know that Mrs Gunn is dead, right?" Walker said.

"I know, it's terrible. Mr Gunn said she fell down the stairs."

"The post-mortem was inconclusive," Macleod said.

"What does that mean?"

"It means that she might have fallen. Or she might have been pushed."

The blood drained from Debbie Macintosh's face. "That can't be right. I mean… She just fell down the stairs. He told me that."

Walker leaned towards her. "Was she often unsteady on her feet? You're a nurse, right? Would you expect her to fall down the stairs? She looked in good health to me when I met her."

She wouldn't meet his eyes. "I don't know."

"Is he worth it? Paul Gunn? This is a serious matter and you're covering up for him."

"I could lose my job," she whispered. "I've got bills and I'll never get something that pays that well again."

"What is it they say about the wages of sin?" Macleod asked severely.

Then she burst into tears.

When Macintosh had got a hold of herself, she started speaking. "I've been working for Mr Gunn for over a year, but he didn't like me talking about it. In fact, it was a condition of the job, that I don't mention it to anyone."

"Tell us about his illness."

"I… I really can't say."

Macleod was losing patience. "Would Huntington's have

261

anything to do with it?"

The woman let out an audible gasp. "No one was supposed to know," she said.

"But you knew," Macleod prompted.

"Yes. Mr Gunn said that they had diagnosed him on holiday in Spain a couple of years ago. He had fallen over in the shower, but there must have been a sharp Doctor on duty because they thought there might be more to it than that. They did the test and it came back positive for Huntington's. And then they gave him all the paperwork to send to his Doctor in the UK. But…"

"But he never gave it to them."

"No."

"Why not?"

"I'm not sure, but he really didn't want anyone to know about it. When I came to work I had to dress normally and then get changed into my uniform when I was already inside. He wanted the neighbours to think I was a cleaner or something. But mainly he wanted someone to pop in, to give him the odd injection or check his bloods. Monitor his medication. It was all basic stuff."

"How did he get the medication?"

Again, she dropped her gaze. "I didn't ask."

Walker shook his head but said nothing. The woman would

have to be reported to the nursing council for this. He would ask Bernie all about it next time he saw her.

"His wife must have known about his condition?"

Macintosh nodded. "She did. I don't think she wanted him to hide it either. I heard them arguing about it a few times. But I guess she went along with what he wanted. It wasn't like he was hurting anyone. I suppose it will all come out now?"

"One way or the other," Macleod said. "Now I would like you to go back to work but please don't tell Mr Gunn that we know about his condition."

"Why not?"

"We wouldn't want to upset him any further, would we?"

"No," she shook her head. "You must be wrong about poor Mrs Gunn. I'm sure she just fell down the stairs."

"I wish I was," Macleod said after the woman had left the room. "If that man is a killer then I don't like the idea of sending the nurse back in with him. Can you get a couple of Constables along to the hotel to keep an eye on him? Call it welfare checks or something."

"Sure," Walker said, already heading for the office.

"Whatever happens we'll bring Gunn in tomorrow morning," Macleod said. "Let's make sure we have a plan before then."

After relaying Macleod's orders to the other members of the team, Walker finally clocked off for the night. It was dark and cold by the time he walked out of the station, with a fine drizzle coating every exposed part of his body.

When he got to his car he spotted a large figure leaning against it, hood pulled low over his brow.

"Hi Ru," Walker said, not sure of the sort of response he was about to receive.

"Can I get in? It's bloody freezing."

"Sure."

They both got in and Walker turned the heaters on so that they steamed the moisture off.

Ru looked like someone had punched him in the face with red eyes and swollen eye sockets. Walker was not overcome with sympathy.

"I screwed up there, didn't I?"

Walker let out a deep breath. "You did."

"Thought I would make things better for you. You seemed so stressed out with everything, and I thought, well maybe I should have a word with this bird that you're crazy about."

"What the hell were you thinking?" Walker said, feeling the anger rise again. "It was none of your business. I mean, I just got this text from you saying that you were heading around to Mary's and by the time I got there... well, you can hardly blame the woman for mace-ing you."

"I know. I screwed up. Do you know it wasn't until I was

264

washing that crud out of my eyes that I really thought about what I was doing? I mean, I thought that I was saving you."

"From being happy?"

Ru shrugged. "That wasn't how I saw it. Look, you're the baby brother. You've always been the odd one out, haven't you? I mean, you barely acknowledge mum and dad."

"There's reasons for that," Walker said from between gritted teeth.

"I get that. Believe me. I thought that you might need someone to stick up for you. You've still got a family you know."

Walker said nothing.

"But then I thought, well, the sort of woman who would pepper spray an attacker in the face, maybe that's just the sort of woman that suits you perfectly. You've never exactly been conventional. I mean, our parents always wanted you to go to Uni, get a normal job, earn lots of money like I do." Ru laughed. "But that would have killed you, wouldn't it?"

"Yeah." It was funny to hear him acknowledge it. "Ru, I spent half my life wanting to be you. Every time you succeeded at anything, mum would throw it back in my face just to show how useless I was. Don't defend her, you know it's true. And I tried so hard to be clever like you, popular like you, but the harder I tried, the more I failed. And then I found the army, but that was just a different kind of failure, trying to be another person that was just... I don't know, like a disguise or

265

something. It's only been in the last few years that I've finally found something I'm actually good at. And Mary is the first person to make all of that better."

Ru let out a short laugh. "And now I'm the screw-up. I thought that Violet was the long term thing, you know? Do you think there's any way she'll take me back?"

Probably not, Walker thought. "Maybe. Got to be worth a try, right?"

Ru looked a bit happier at that idea. "I'll head back down the road tomorrow and see if she'll let me back in. Besides, your place is far too small."

"You're not wrong," Walker said, giving him a smile. He started the car, glad that they had at least cleared the air, even if there was always a chance of another argument.

But he was happy to have a temporary truce. Like that bit in the First World War where everyone stopped fighting for Christmas and had a football match instead. Of course, they went back to shooting and bayonetting each other the next day, but at least they got to enjoy a bit of Christmas pudding.

Chapter 41: Bernie

First thing on Friday morning Bernie made sure her phone wasn't on silent. She knew it was just a matter of time before she got a call from the police station. She went for a shower with her phone balanced on the shelf above the sink – why do they make these so tiny – then cooked up an egg-white omelette with her phone on the countertop.

By ten o'clock she was starting to doubt herself. When Finn had left to drop Ewan at school and head to work, she had confidently told him that she would be at the police station before long. Her self-confidence, normally unshakeable, was beginning to waver after she had made her third cup of black coffee.

At ten twenty-five the phone rang.

"You're late," Bernie said.

"What do you mean," Mary's voice came from the other end. "I don't think I was meant to call you, was I?"

"Oh, I thought you were someone else," Bernie said, trying not to sound too disappointed. "You came up on my phone as an unknown number."

"That's because I'm at the police station. They want you to come over right away."

"Yes!" Bernie punched the air. "I knew it. Give me five

minutes and I'll be right there."

"Can you bring me something to eat? I didn't get a chance to have breakfast. Not anything with the word 'protein' on it, please."

Bernie looked in the cupboard. "That doesn't leave much. What about the cheese snack packs that I get for Ewan's packed lunches."

"That'll do," Mary said happily. "I'll see you soon."

A quick car journey later Bernie was sitting in Superintendent MacKinnon's office with DI Macleod, Walker and Mary. It was quite a squeeze and the strong smell of cheese and processed meat slices from Mary's direction wasn't helping with Bernie's feelings of claustrophobia.

"Can I just say that I have grave reservations about your plan, Inspector," MacKinnon was giving Macleod a penetrating stare.

"I know. But I've been going back and forth all morning about this. At the moment, there is just not enough evidence to suggest that Mrs Gunn's death was anything other than an accident. We've got forensics back at the house again today to try and find something, but so far they are drawing a blank."

Macleod pulled a caramel wafer out of his pocket and started eating it. Between him and Mary with her children's snack pack, Bernie was seriously thinking about staging an intervention.

"That's why we need to think outside the box," Walker said.

"Bernie was the one that saved his life that day up on the stage. That gives her the perfect reason to go and speak to him."

"And the word 'entrapment' is not relevant here?"

"Entrapment is part of Scottish law thanks to the incorporation of the European Convention on Human Rights," Mary said, pausing mid-munch. Every person in the room looked at her. "What? I like to research these things. Besides, entrapment is only a problem if it causes someone to create a crime, not to confess to one, which I'm sure the Superintendent is aware of."

Four pairs of eyes swivelled back to MacKinnon, who cleared his throat. "I was, ah, using the term colloquially. What I meant was that we don't want any confession or anything else he says to be inadmissible as evidence."

Mary nodded sagely. "Secret recordings can be admissible in court, but it would ultimately come down to the judge."

MacKinnon did not look like he was enjoying this one bit, but Macleod interrupted before Mary could say anything else.

"Even if we can't use anything we record directly at trial," Macleod explained. "We are hoping to get some pointers on his wife's death. We might at least find out if he had a reason to kill her. Or if he was even capable of doing it."

MacKinnon clicked his pen. "Fine. Get out of my sight. But if this all goes wrong, I want my objection to be noted."

Classic arse-covering, Bernie thought, but for once she didn't challenge him on it. She knew it was luck and Macleod's good graces that were letting them anywhere near this investigation in the first place.

They drove over to the hotel in the police van, which was rather fun. Bernie hadn't been in the back of one since the Iraq war protests when she might or might not have done something naughty with a traffic cone.

"And you know the script, Ms Paterson," Macleod said for the third time. "Don't try and goad him into anything or he'll probably clam up. This is a guy who has kept a major illness secret from everyone for several years. He's not about to make silly mistakes."

Bernie nodded. The Inspector seemed nervous, but she was feeling confident. If she had let herself be intimidated by grumpy old men lying in bed then she wouldn't have lasted five minutes in the care home. She would make sure that Paul Gunn confessed to his wife's murder. She just hadn't quite worked out how yet.

When they got to the hotel, Macleod went first to speak to the nurse, Debbie Macintosh. Bernie didn't trust herself to hold a conversation with the woman. Happy to give her patient whatever medication he asked for and not question where he got it: to Bernie's mind that was negligent. The police officers had promised her that the woman would be reported once the case was complete, and for the moment Bernie had to accept that.

Macintosh led them upstairs to the suite where Paul Gunn had been installed. After a lot of whispered discussion outside the door, she agreed to let them see her patient.

270

"We want Bernie to go in and chat to him," Walker explained. "She's the one that performed CPR on your employer at the Cook-Off. He owes her his life."

"The woman with the resting bitch face?" Macintosh returned Bernie's glare. "She doesn't seem like an angel of mercy to me."

Mary put her hand on Bernie's arm, so she managed to clamp her jaw shut.

"Do you think Mr Gunn will agree to see her?"

"He really needs to rest."

"I think it might do you some good if you persuade him to see her," Macleod said, his usual light-hearted tone turning stern. "After all, we don't know quite how far you are implicated in all of this."

Now it was Macintosh's turn to put on a sour expression. "I'll see what I can do."

She disappeared behind the door for a few minutes, then returned.

"He says he'll see the woman. I told him she wanted to see how he was getting on. I didn't mention the rest of you."

"Good work." He turned to Bernie. "Right, we've already set your phone to record the conversation. You don't have to do anything to it, just talk normally. Let's see what he has to say."

Bernie nodded. She was slightly disappointed that she wasn't

271

'wearing a wire', but apparently mobile phones were cheaper and easier. Bernie missed the old days of police work, even if they had only really existed on the telly.

"Mr Gunn?" When Bernie went into the room the lamps were turned down low and the curtains were shut. The very idea offended her nurse's soul.

"Shall I open the curtains, let the air circulate?"

"No thank you," a weak voice said from the bed. "I'd rather those vermin photographers from the tabloids weren't able to look in. They've been sniffing around all week."

"Really? I haven't seen any. Maybe you're not as famous as you think," Bernie added.

Paul Gunn's head wobbled a little. "I thought you wanted to speak to me? Debbie said you did."

"Oh, yes," Bernie remembered she was meant to be playing a part. "The thing is, I was there when you collapsed on stage. I'm a nurse, you see."

"Just like Debbie."

"Uh huh," Bernie was proud of herself for not rising to that one. "I wanted you to know what happened while you were unconscious. You know, the CPR and everything. A lot of people worry about these things."

"Thank you," Paul Gunn said, breaking into a smile. "It was a bit of a worry. I can't remember anything about it."

"Do you remember taking the medication that day? And having a few drinks?"

The smile disappeared. "Are you implying it was my fault? You do know that someone spiked my coffee."

"So I heard. But... hang on, let me check something." Bernie took a notebook out of her handbag. "Ah, yes, here it is. According to the testimony of One-shot Sam he only put one pill into your cup. But there was a lot more benzodiazepine than you would get in one pill."

"How do you know all this? Who are you?"

"Oh, didn't I say? I'm a private investigator. And I want to know about what happened to your wife."

Did Bernie imagine it or was there a faint groan from the corridor?

"My wife? She fell down the stairs," Gunn shuffled up the bed. "Where is my nurse?"

"The lovely Debbie is having a little break," Bernie said. "But don't worry, I'm fully qualified."

She put the notebook down on the table next to the window. "I don't suppose you've left any medication lying about here that I could check up on. You wouldn't want to be taking the wrong things, would you? Especially as you're not suffering from anything other than a cardiac incident, right?"

Gunn said nothing, just watched her prowl around the room with his brows lowered.

"I'll just have a peek in the bathroom if you don't mind. Check all the accessibility features are there. We wouldn't want you to keel over in the shower now, would we?"

Bernie spent a few minutes pretending to fiddle with the taps and the shower curtain before coming back into the room.

"I know what you were thinking," Paul Gunn sniffed. "If you wander around and leave that notepad over there then I will jump out of bed and look at it and you'll catch me in the act. I may be getting on a bit, but I've not taken leave of my senses just yet."

"Oh, I knew you wouldn't go for that," Bernie smiled. "I was trying to find something. I thought it was over here, but it turns out it was under the bed."

She held up a small black box.

"It's a camera. I had a friend of mine place it under the bed here yesterday. Remember the cleaner that you shouted at for not ironing the pillowcases? That was her."

"What? You can't do that!"

"Do you remember filling in a lot of forms when you checked in here? Whoever looks at these things, right? Well, you probably should have checked these ones. Because you signed a form saying that you were happy for all audio and video recordings to be used that were taken in this room."

"That's just a trick!"

Bernie laughed. "Of course, but it's a trick that we can take a firm bet on at court. Now, what is this camera going to show? I'll bet that you're a hell of a lot more mobile than you've been making out."

"You evil little…" Gunn lunged out of the bed, getting to his feet remarkably quickly for someone who should be resting.

The door to the room burst open.

"Settle down, sir," Inspector Macleod said.

Paul Gunn collapsed back into the bed. "That woman aggravated me. It doesn't prove anything."

"Not by itself," Walker replied. "But it is rather suggestive."

"We put a hand grenade in the room, you see," Mary gestured at Bernie. "And we knew it was only a matter of time before you reacted."

"I prefer nuclear bomb to hand grenade," Bernie said.

"Of course you do."

Chapter 42: Mary

It was strange, Mary thought, to look back at the first time she had seen Paul Gunn at the Cook-Off. At first, he had seemed like your average veteran broadcaster, playing up to the crowd and getting everyone laughing. Then when he had collapsed, he had looked like an old man, vulnerable and weak. And now he looked like something quite different. No longer harmless, despite the fact he was in bed, his eyes as he watched them were shrewd and calculating. Mary was pretty sure she was looking at a murderer. Now they just had to find enough evidence to take him to court.

"You need to delete that footage," Gunn was saying to Bernie. "It's an invasion of my privacy."

"Maybe, maybe not," Macleod said. "It's a grey area for the courts."

Mary gave Paul Gunn a flash of her dimples. "We wanted to know how good your mobility was. If you were able to get up and around the hotel room, then it seems to me that you wouldn't have a problem pushing your wife down the stairs. Is that what the camera will show us?"

"Just because I can get around and… do certain activities, doesn't mean that I could murder anyone."

"Certain activities?" Mary put her hand to her mouth. "OMG, have you been 'doing' the nurse?"

While Paul Gunn turned a shade of purplish-red, Bernie burst out laughing.

"We've got a Dirty Beggar mark two!"

Walker cleared his throat. "All right, ladies. I'm afraid, Mr Gunn, that any relationship with your nurse doesn't make it sound like you were grieving for your wife."

"It's none of your business."

"What was our business was some missing evidence at the Cook-Off."

Gunn frowned. "Now you're clutching at straws. You know that that had nothing to do with me. That was Petty and his bitter feud."

"That's right, but it did help us learn some things. Did you know that Nevyn Petty had enlisted the help of a Special Police Constable?"

"No."

"I'm afraid the man was paid to remove the cup that you had drunk from. The Special in question will be disciplined, don't you worry. He told us he left the evidence bag in the boot of his car. But as it turned out, the interesting thing was that our man hadn't mentioned the other evidence he had taken. Because Nevyn was so worried about someone finding out about the prank, he had asked the Special to take the rest of the pills from your bag. So we have clear evidence that you have been obtaining the benzodiazepine without a prescription."

"Hardly the sort of crime worth bothering the police about."

"No. But finding the pills did teach us some interesting things. First of all, whose name was on the prescription? It was your wife's name, not yours, wasn't it?"

Paul Gunn's eyes narrowed, but he didn't reply.

"The name on the prescription is Emily Gunn. That was your wife's name, right?"

Gunn looked like he was choosing his words carefully. "Again, I don't think that prescription fraud is exactly the biggest worry for Police Scotland, is it? Even if you could prove it. It's not exactly something to bother the courts over."

"But murder is."

"Why would I kill my wife? Emily has been nothing but supportive of me for forty years."

Mary couldn't help but let her emotion show. "That's why it's so awful. She was willing to keep your secret for so long, but when she finally decided she had had enough, you killed her."

"Pure speculation."

"Not entirely," Walker said. "We were chatting with your nurse Debbie outside just a minute ago. She had mentioned before that you and your wife had argued about keeping the Huntington's quiet. And funnily enough, now that she's looking at being prosecuted herself, she's remembered some other things. Your wife didn't know about your secret daughter, did she?"

Paul Gunn pressed his lips shut, but Walker just kept talking.

"I reckon she had no idea that you had fathered a child with Nevyn Petty's wife until it all came out after the Cook-Off. She had put up with just about everything, but a secret child was the last straw."

"No proof," Paul Gunn repeated, like a bad robot from an early Doctor Who episode, all tin foil and glitter.

"We do know that your wife was ready to expose you," Mary said. "She called her GP the day before she died. The GP told us that she wanted to stop her prescription, that she was feeling much better. She had finally had enough, hadn't she, Mr Gunn."

Gunn's mouth opened and shut twice, but then he spoke in a low voice. "I... We argued. If she told anyone about the Huntington's, I could kiss my career goodbye. I was under such a lot of stress. I don't really remember what happened. You know that I'm on these strong painkillers. I think we were arguing, and then she fell."

Mary glanced at Walker who gave her a small nod. That was probably as close to a confession as they were going to get. She felt sick from the sight of the murderer lying in the bed.

"I'm going to get some air," Mary said, leaving the room and walking outside. It was blowing a hoolie, but it was preferable to that tiny room with the liar in the bed.

"Are you all right?" Walker asked when he came out a few minutes later.

Bernie joined them and gave her arm a squeeze. "You did good in there."

"Thanks. So did you."

Walker fixed her scarf which was in danger of flying away. "Macleod is going to arrange custody for Paul Gunn. We've got enough to charge him with murder."

"If they can't prove 'mens rea' then it'll be culpable homicide rather than murder, I should think," Mary said. "If Paul Gunn can prove there was no 'wicked intent to kill' then it's not going to meet the requirements to be tried as a murder case."

"What am I paying you at the moment?" Bernie asked.

"Two quid more an hour than when I was just doing the admin."

"I'm going to give you a raise," she said.

"Thanks. Can I have an advance of a cup of tea and a bit of cake?"

"Just this once," Bernie grinned. "Next time it's a salad."

Chapter 43: Alice

Alice had never felt such relief as she had when One-shot Sam and Nevyn Petty had been ruled out of the murder investigation. It meant that her failure to report the video to the station had not been the reason for the poor woman's death. But she knew she was still right to resign. When it mattered, Alice had chosen the WWC over the police, and that was clear for all to see.

Now they were all at Mary's place for a celebration. Little Lauren who was recovering better than anyone expected had been allowed to visit her grandmother and for once Mary's house was child-free. Which was lucky as otherwise there was no way that they would have all fitted into the tiny living room.

As it was, Alice and Bernie were sitting on bean bags, while a rather uneasy-looking Inspector Macleod was slumped on the sofa. He had the look of someone who had ended up in the enemy's lair, but he was busying himself looking through Mary's DVD collection.

"Is that the original *Cracker*?" he asked.

"Yeah, every episode," Mary replied. "You can borrow it if you like."

"Cheers."

Walker had turned up with a large man who kept rubbing his eyes.

"This is my brother, Ruaridh, but everyone calls him Ru."

"Oh aye, I heard all about you," Bernie said, placing her hands on her hips.

Uh oh, Alice thought, Bernie's on the warpath. Again.

"You did?" Ru gave Walker his best glare. "I thought we'd agreed never to mention it again."

"Don't look at me," Walker said. "The woman has a network of spies."

Ru coughed. "I'm here to apologise to Mary. From everything I've heard, she sounds like a... well, a decent girlfriend for my brother. I shouldn't have tried to interfere."

"Apology accepted," Mary said.

Liz moved along a space so that Ru could perch on the end of the sofa. Baby Isioma was fast asleep on Bernie's shoulder who so far hadn't let anyone else have a turn. Not that Alice had been looking for one. She had never understood the fascination with babies and their germy little faces.

"A toast!" Liz said, holding out a glass of fizz. "To solving the case and to our newest recruit, Alice Paterson!"

Alice shook her head while the others cheered. "What are you talking about? I'm not a recruit."

"Well, I know that you've been working for us every so often, but Bernie said that you had quit the police to join us full time. I reckon that qualifies as a recruit."

"Bernie told you that, did she?" Alice looked at her aunt.

"I didn't realise it was a secret."

"It's not a secret. It's not true. Yes, I've quit the Specials, but I'm not going to join the WWC. In fact, I'm not going to be around at all."

"What on earth are you talking about?" Bernie grunted.

Alice sighed. She had planned to tell her aunt in private, but as usual with Bernie, nothing ever went to plan.

"I've signed up for a teaching program in China. I've been thinking about doing something different for ages, I just couldn't decide what. I'll be working with college students, and I'll be an assistant in the photography department at a local university, so I can use my degree. I applied for it before, I just hadn't decided whether or not to take it. I'll be leaving next month."

There was a moment of silence while everyone in the room digested the news.

"Congratulations," Mary said, pulling her into a bear hug. "I'm so happy for you. I would have loved to do something like that at your age."

Bernie came over, a frown wrinkling her forehead. "I guess it's a good thing," she said reluctantly. "I mean, it's not what I would do, but it's what you would do, so it'll probably be fine."

"Thanks," Alice said, knowing that was as close as she was going to get to a 'good choice'.

"More fizz!" Liz said, clearly enjoying the fact that she was no longer pregnant. "Looks like we're having a party."

Several hours later everyone was a little the worse for wear. Inspector Macleod had slunk away after one beer. Alice reckoned he hadn't particularly enjoyed Mary's choice of music which only seemed to range from 1987 to 1998.

Bernie, not normally a big drinker, had had a few gins and had somehow managed to corner Mary and Walker outside on the patio. Alice thought she might go and see if anyone needed help.

"You know, you better treat my friend right," Bernie was saying as Alice stepped out through the patio doors.

"Oh god," Mary covered her eyes.

Bernie was doing that drunk pointing thing, wagging her finger in Walker's face. "She's already had to suffer ten years with one feckless husband and I won't let her take on another."

"I'm not feckless," Walker objected. "I've got lots of fecks."

"What is a feck anyway?" Alice asked, trying to lighten the mood.

"A leather harness for a ferret," Bernie said quickly. She would never have admitted to not knowing something. "Anyway, that's beside the point. The point is that you've got a good woman there. One of the best. Even if she is a wet lettuce. And I don't want you stomping in here with your police-issue boots and messing everything up."

Walker puffed out his chest. "Bernadette Paterson, I have no intention of messing anything up. Mary is going to be my partner for the rest of my life. Make no mistake, whatever you or my brother or anyone says about it."

Bernie raised an eyebrow. "Was that a proposal?"

"What? No!" Walker shrunk back down to normal size. "When I propose it will not be in front of Mary's annoying boss, that's for sure."

"Did you, um, say when you propose?" Mary asked.

Bernie tapped her foot. "And another thing –"

"There's a bug in your hair, Bernie," Alice said.

Bernie turned to face her, hands on hips. "How the hell do you know about that?"

"Uncle Finn told me. Said he had a funny feeling that I might need to say it to you today at some point."

"Well, I happen to think that is the most outrageous abuse of power," Bernie said, giving her a force ten glare. "And you needn't think that just because you're moving to the other end of the world you can get away with any of your nonsense."

"Auntie?"

"Yes."

"Give us a hug," Alice said, pulling Bernie into an embrace. Her aunt permitted her to squeeze her for almost ten seconds.

285

"Another gin?" Bernie asked when she managed to wriggle free.

"Why not," Alice said. "It's not time to go yet."

Afterword

Thank you so much for reading the latest in the Wronged Women's Co-operative series. This was a bit more emotional to write then most. The idea of having a poorly child, whether viral meningitis or something much worse, is something every parent dreads. I'm terrible for googling every rash and nappy change, and I don't think modern technology and having a phone in my hand constantly has helped with my parental anxiety!

Thankfully I have the lovely ladies of the WWC to cheer me up. When I'm writing these novels, even in the serious sections, I know it won't be too long before Bernie is making inappropriate remarks or Mary is drooling over a pistachio éclair. People can sometimes be a little dismissive of the cosier side of crime fiction, but I think now more than ever we need a little light to stave off the darkness. I hope you feel the same.

The next book in the series is available to order from amazon now.

Printed in Dunstable, United Kingdom

77418370R00163